BEST *Lesbian* LOVE STORIES

2010

BEST Lesbian LOVE STORIES

2010

edited by
SIMONE THORNE

ALYSON books

Best Lesbian Love Stories 2010
Edited by Simone Thorne

Published by Alyson Books
245 West 17th Street, Suite 1200, New York, NY 10011
www.alyson.com

ALYSONbooks

All rights reserved. No part of this book may be reproduced in whole or in part without written permission from the publisher, except by reviewers who may quote brief excerpts in connection with a review in a newspaper, magazine or electronic publication; nor may any part of this book be reproduced, stored in a retrieval system, or transmitted in any form or by any means electronic, mechanical, photocopying, recording, or other without written permission from the publisher.

Copyright © 2009 by Alyson Books.

First Edition: June 2009

10 9 8 7 6 5 4 3 2 1

ISBN-10: 1-59350-109-9
ISBN-13: 978-1-59350-109-9

Library of Congress Cataloging-in-Publication data are on file.

Cover design by Victor Mingovits

Printed in the United States of America
Distributed by Consortium Book Sales and Distribution
Distribution in the United Kingdom by Turnaround Publisher Services Ltd.

CONTENTS

INTRODUCTION vii

GOLDEN LOTUS BY JACQUELINE CRAIGIE 1

IN THE SUMMER BED BY QUINN GABRIEL 9

A TRUE AWAKENING BY PAM GALLIEN 19

OPENING NIGHT BY CHARLOTTE DARE 33

TOUR OF DUTY BY T. LEE 47

THE COLLISION OF COASTS BY AIMEE HERMAN 57

S.O.A.R. BY JOY PARKS 67

MISFIRE BY LORI HICKS 81

THE ASHES OF SHANGIRL-LA BY GENEVA NIXON 93

WHITE SHOULDERS BY JANET WILLIAMS 99

THE TRAIN RIDE HOME BY ANGELA L. RECKLEIN 111

SO MUCH TO DISCOVER BY BETSY CONNOLLY 123

TWO-WAY LOVE STORY (HER COUCH IS WIDE) BY NICKI REED 137

I HEART YOU BY KISSA STARLING 151

STEPPING OUT BY J W HARNISCH 163

CALLIE'S LOVE STORY BY MERINA CANYON 179

**THE TALE OF A LESBIAN SLUT: HOW I MET AND MARRIED
A NICE JEWISH DOCTOR** *(MY MOTHER IS SO PROUD!)*,
OR, HOW I BECAME MONOGAMOUS AND MARRIED BY TATE O'BRIEN 201

INTRODUCTION

A SHATTERED HEART is worthless and in my opinion, one of the reasons why love has become theatrical these past years. You've seen it in the theater or a television show: Some poor unsuspecting couple has a slight misunderstanding and they break off their romance, leaving them both disillusioned with not only each other, but with love. This, in my opinion, is only a fundamental understanding of the trials of love. True love is expansion, a metamorphosis that constantly changes. Sometimes it is anger, bliss, and even skepticism. Other times it's so raw and undefined, it's hard to swallow. This is true love, and this is what I believe in.

Even if love fell apart, no superglue to hold it together, you still learned something from that experience. This experience is the source of love but more importantly, the spark that has kept it going for eons. Everyone always forgets that love is passion and passion can sometimes go wayward. However, no matter how disastrous, you still need to believe in the love you have. Whether your night with your lover ends with two red lipstick marks on two champagne glasses or a heated argument that involves throwing things, this is the source of your love: growing and experiencing things together and overcoming every obstacle in your way.

The stories in this anthology reflect all of this. The women represented in this collection have written about love and how they've overcome all in their way. There may not always be a happy ending, but they walk away richer and far more experienced.

Yours,
Simone Thorne

BEST
Lesbian
LOVE STORIES

2010

GOLDEN LOTUS

JACQUELINE CRAIGIE

HEATHER AWOKE AND realized that there could be more than what she had in life. Unfulfilled, she dropped out of law school and became a landscape gardener. Fingers deep in the dirt, she controlled her life and manipulated seasons. It was never any surprise to find tulips in the crunch of winter or orchids in the blister of summer.

She used to categorize people as differing varieties of flowers. "You'd be a Golden Lotus," she would say to me. I'd never seen a Golden Lotus so I was afraid that I'd been either complimented or ridiculed. When I asked over and over again what a Golden Lotus was like, she'd smile and tell me that there was no point asking a Banksia.

I thought of her after that as a beautiful Banksia. Even to this day when I smell the pungent scent of the Banksia blossom, or when I see the gnarled branches elbowing the sky, I imagine Heather. I think she chose the Banksia to represent herself because it only ever flowered after it had been set alight. The pod that encases the seeds needs the ravages of fire and singeing of heat to make it give forth. I imagined her as the phoenix of flowers, barren, burnt; fertile, born again.

We read poetry in the warm womb of her house. Each lamp was adorned with thin material draped across the globe to create her atmosphere. She had skin the color of chocolate yet she smelled like the ocean. Always I would find flower petals, leaves, and bark in the web of her fine hair. I dreamt I kissed her deeply, knowing as I always knew, that she'd taste like honey and jasmine. Her skin was salty on my tongue, her mouth hungry.

I awoke on my birthday to a garden bed full of sunflowers, giant heads nodding in the breeze. They seemed to be greeting me, smiling hello. I walked across to her back door (we were neighbors) with the intention of thanking her, of slipping my hands up the length of her back and into her hair. I was determined to feel her hips pressed into mine. She came to the door and reduced me to nerves with her smile and I couldn't bear to bare my soul to her. She offered me tea and we planned a night watching a meteor shower.

Sometimes I could hear her music drifting into my bedroom across the driveway we shared. Other times I could hear her in the depths of night making love to someone from a nightclub somewhere.

In summer we walked to the botanical gardens in the city so she could show me her passions. I knew already what they were but humored her anyway. On the way there, she described the first time she saw me as I moved in next door. By the amount of white goods that came out of the moving van, she guessed I was either a young corporate yuppie type, or a single parent. She was horrified at sharing a driveway with a banker or an accountant. Then she saw my car. It was a beat up Cortina, so holey that I began raising daisies in the back seat. I loved opening the car door to a sea of flowers. She nicknamed my car "Daisy Chain."

Whenever we walked anywhere she would reel off the names of any Australian natives that we passed. "That's a

Leptospermum flavescens, a lemon tea tree," she would say as she pulled off a few leaves, slowly grinding them into the palm of her hand before offering me their smell. The tangy lemon was fresh and sweet. She would drop the leaves and rub the oil over her neck. Later in the day when we shared hot chips by the Brisbane River, I could smell the fine tincture of lemon in the air.

After Anzac Day, we lay in King George Square as the litter from a thousand marigolds lay about us. As I drifted off from exhaustion and peace I heard her whisper, "How beautiful." Then she threw great handfuls of orange and yellow into the air. The riot of broken marigolds snowed down, settling like dust over our bodies. She laughed at my deep sighs. Kiss me, I thought over and over again. My mantra fell on deaf ears. She rolled on her side and talked of nature and beauty. I only saw her.

In winter we went jogging in the evenings. Running beside me I could hear her breathe. I could hear her steady pace. Sometimes our sweaty arms would collide and slip and glide against one another. It set my heart racing and a slow ache would seep out from my core but she never seemed to notice.

Heather was vegan and only drank soy milk. At 6:00 a.m. on my back deck, she would come over empty handed and ask if I wanted to go to the shops with her for soy milk. We always drove because the only twenty-four-hour organic shop was in Red Hill. When we got there it was coffee first at the café next door. Talk came later, and soy milk was last. She was sensual in a coffee shop and I felt embarrassed at the eroticism of her movements. Her wet mouth, the way her tongue greeted the thick rim of the mug, and her slow and deliberate licking of her lips. I ordered chamomile tea.

She would inevitably take a sip of mine as well. I remained calm. She always forgot the soy milk.

When the chill lifted and winter bled into spring, we sat on the front deck and drank peppermint tea. Heather took hers with a dash of cold water; I preferred mine steaming hot. I enjoyed the torturous pleasure of waiting for it in its own time. I would even prolong the drink because she was polite enough to stay in my company until I was finished. We left the tea bags in with the tabs dangling over the edge. They were little lifelines between our minty Brisbane and fields of tea sweating on the other side of the globe. Peppermint Patty starred in one of our conversations. What a wonderful heroine Heather thought she was, a feminist poster child.

We planted an herb garden after turning out the soil. I could smell the earth between my fingers. Coriander, mint, parsley, and lemongrass rubbed shoulders with one another, crowding for position. She surprised me with rosemary and basil cuttings from her own garden, a little piece of her in my front yard.

We knelt by each other as we planted, dirty knees, sunburnt foreheads. I rocked back on my heels and admired her dedication. She made deliberate holes in the ground before carefully tapping the herbs out of their pots. Ever so gently her fingers teased and tickled out the roots, freeing them to explore their new homes. When she turned on the hose, the water came out thick and warm, smelling like rubber. The clay-rich soil swelled and pulsated with water, pooling at the base of each plant where she had dug tiny moats to trap goodness. The water percolated and bubbled, like the coffee Heather loved so much, then drained suddenly away, leaving a sledge of disarrayed leaves and twigs on the black surface.

She found another lover so I tended to the garden by myself. She was so consumed by passion and overwhelmed by lust that her cat, Necromancer, came to me, neglected. At night I heard her, happy and fulfilled. The reek of jasmine scented the air. I tortured myself by placing bunches of it throughout the house.

I came home one day to find Heather in my kitchen, looking for Necromancer, crying. I held her while she sobbed and I made peppermint tea to soothe her soul. It didn't work because she was changed. Nothing was the same for her anymore. She had the taste of bitterness in her veins and everything was sour. I asked her what plant her lover had been and she told me that no plant would do, that her lover had been her fire. I held my breath because it hurt to see her so upset.

She slept in my arms that night and I sinned against her mourning and loss by wanting her more than ever. I couldn't sleep for the fear that my dreams would sneak out of my control and creep their sordid way into reality. I watched her as sleep took her to a restless place. I held her hand tentatively and drifted off nervously sometime before sunrise.

We sat that morning out the back of the house as summer walked up the driveway to greet us. Small beads of sweat gathered on her top lip, threatening to escape but remaining vigilantly on guard. "I love summer," she exclaimed and I always agreed.

"Of course we do," Heather said, "because you are a Golden Lotus and I am a Banksia. We want for the same things."

I wondered why she didn't think of me as a daisy, like the ones growing in my car, masters of opportunity, or as the sunflowers that she planted for me, bright faced and eternally optimistic. I planned to research the Golden Lotus that day in the library. I knew it would feel good to be surrounded by cool concrete, dust, and dank books on such a hot day. I wanted to ask her why I was a lotus but was still afraid of the answer. Either way, it seemed exotic, something I feared I was not.

The library was my garden—beds of books lined up—but not on that particular day. Instead, Heather insisted that we spend the day at the beach but because of my daisy-infested car, we took hers instead.

Her car seemed none other than an extension of herself. It was a Valiant, and I thought her so, valiant that is. Courageous, brave, sensual. What else could she drive? Maybe a Lanos? The Greek word for *beautiful*. But without the classic feel, it would never have suited her. She had used her own hands to massage that car into shape. We argued over the color. She said it was white; I saw pale tints of green. We surveyed friends and mechanics, adding to our arguments. Eventually she acquiesced when the registration papers proclaimed that it was colored pale green. She brought them to me, evidence that she was honest.

We drove with music blaring, windows down. The wind buffeted our faces and whipped our hair into knots. She rolled cigarettes with one hand, the other on the steering wheel. The small pink of her tongue darted out to wet the paper. I looked away. The vinyl seats grew sweaty and hot beneath our skin. An image of her in slow motion remains etched in my mind. She is driving and concentrating. I say something and almost languidly she turns her face to me and smiles; a flash of brilliance. She drives straight backed, leaning slightly forward in her seat so that her body never quite touches the seat.

The sand is hot, blistering in fact. Heather tells me to bring my towel closer to hers. Touch me, I beg silently, touch me. She runs her hand through her hair and lies back. Her body is contoured and strong from gardening and sport. Her skin is the color of caramel. We enter the water laughing at the possibility of sharks. As she dips under a wave, I see pale white edging out beneath her bathers and a thrill goes through me. Embarrassed, I wet my hair and let the tiny shards of icy water trickle torturously down my hot back.

On the beach, salt dries on her eyelashes in miniature sparkling crystals. "Shall we go?" she asks as the sun begins to feel as if it might scald us. I want to stay; I want the possibility. Beneath my fingers there are a million tiny spiral shells. I grab a handful and let them slip out like an hourglass. I tell her that I think that they are amazingly perfect, just like this summer day. She picks one up and studies it. "Yes, they are magnificent," she says and then she swallows one. The beach becomes a part of her.

We track slowly up the sand, towels and feet dragging. She places a spare towel over the boiling vinyl seat so that we won't burn our tender skin. On the silent drive back, we stop at the strawberry farm and buy a sundae each. It tastes like a strawberry daiquiri, without the sin. I want the sin.

Every Saturday of summer we make the pilgrimage to the sea.

Summer then smudges into autumn and she comes across to my house. "I'm going to Canada," she announces casually. "Isn't it wonderful?" she asks without looking at me. The air sucks out of the room and the brilliance of autumn fades. Her ex wants her back and has bought her a ticket to jet her to the other side of the world and into her arms.

"Yes, of course I will take care of Necromancer. No problem," I say. Even through the pain of it I smile and think: At least this way I know I will see her again. She will come back to me.

She doesn't write me letters. Instead she sends me postcards depicting flowers and plants from different parts of the world. I pin them up on my kitchen wall and look at her traveling garden each morning as I burn my toast and sip my single tea. It too becomes my new garden. I neglect the herbs the way she neglected me. I find pale versions of Heather all over Brisbane. I date them; I sleep with them. I remember.

Necromancer runs away, so I ring and tell her. She doesn't seem upset. She acts as if she knew it was inevitable. She doesn't care the way she should. So I move to London. In my first winter, ice coats everything, including my heart. Various women chip away at it but it keeps layering upon me, thicker and more comforting than before. I think of Heather's Banksia and its need of fire to survive. I stay in icy London. I stay isolated.

Eventually, I hear through friends that they broke up, that Heather is back in Australia. I hear she is back studying law, she wears a suit, her garden is overgrown, and I can't imagine it. I send her postcards of the flowers and plants of the UK. She sends one back and writes, "Even amidst the most fierce flames, the Golden Lotus can be planted." My heart blooms. I want to burn, to ignite.

I reply that I am missing a huge part of myself, my fire. She never replies—her silence deafening.

I am left tending my garden of memories.

IN THE SUMMER BED

QUINN GABRIEL

THE SUMMER WE both turned eighteen, Erin and I decided not to go on vacation with our parents. In a ridiculous move of independence we had volunteered to stay home with the younger siblings and let the two couples go on a child-free getaway. Erin and I had grown up best friends and our mothers were best friends. The Chases could always be found in our backyard for cookouts, at Christmas open houses, and at Fourth of July fireworks displays. Every year, we went somewhere sunny together. Somewhere where there was a beach and fishing and cheap food available from ice cream trucks parked on the sand.

This year we didn't want to go. We would babysit and they would pay us. For me, that meant watching my ten-year-old brother, Kenny, and my twelve-year-old sister, Christie. Poor Erin; she had seven-year-old twins, Jessica and Jeannie, and a surly eleven-year-old brother, Phillip.

It took us about twenty-four hours to realize we had made a horrible mistake. Our parents were out basking in the sun in Florida while we fought with a brood of hot, grumpy kids over change for the ice cream man.

"What have we done?" Erin snorted, shoving a jar of change at the pack of wolves.

"Made our first adult mistake," I said. Then I yelled to Kenny, "Don't forget to get me a red, white, and blue!"

"Fuck," she said.

I shushed her but laughed. "Fuck is right. It's going to be a long week. A long, long week."

"But we're getting paid."

The throng of kids moved toward us and the ice cream man shouted, "You still owe me seventy-five cents."

I dug in my pockets and found some more change. "God. Not enough. We should have asked for double that."

◆

WE HAD DECIDED to camp out at my house for the night. All five siblings were down in the club basement watching *The Love Boat* and presumably behaving. What was almost sure they were doing was torturing each other and throwing popcorn and possibly looking through my dad's album collection.

Erin and I were sprawled out on the sofa upstairs watching the same show. It wasn't so much an issue of television program, it was more: we were eighteen and did not need to watch the goings-on of love and hookups on the high seas with a bunch of little kids.

It was hot. Hotter than hot and I had been instructed to not run the air-conditioning unless it hit ninety-eight degrees. It had hit ninety-seven. The humidity, I was certain, was about 200 percent. I would cheat and turn it on but my father would definitely check his collection of newspapers from the week they were away. Then I would be caught in the snare of his obsessive nature when he found we were a degree short of death.

"That Julie is such a slut," Erin said, nodding at the TV. She was sucking on an Otter Pop. My favorite flavor, Sir Isaac Lime.

I stole it and bit off a chunk.

"Oh, my god! You are not supposed to bite them! No biting. You are supposed to suck them until they go soft and then you can eat them slowly."

"Funny," I said, "I thought you were supposed to suck them until they got hard." I kicked my leg repeatedly, lounging back on the sofa. I would kick it high and let it fall. Anything to relieve the boredom. A one-woman Rockettes show. "It is so fucking hot."

We were in our shorty pajamas. The earmark of summer in the suburbs. Pinstriped or polka-dotted seersucker pajamas. And who the hell thought seersucker would be good? It's hot as hell. "Take off your pajamas," Erin said, finishing her frozen pop. She set the wrapper on the coffee table.

"Babysitting naked. Somehow I don't see that as a good idea." I laughed.

"You are such a prude, Kim. Prude. Although, I bet that weirdo who lives behind you would get an eyeful. You know damn well he watches you with binoculars when he can. Sits in his garage and watches you in your summer pj's and jerks off." She mimicked a guy masturbating furiously and I fell back laughing.

"He does not!" I shrieked. Only, truth be told, I thought he did. Steve was nice enough. Tall and lanky, kind of dorky, but nice and very smart. And he didn't do a damn thing for me although my mother kept trying to set us up. *I can't believe you two didn't do prom together. I mean, Kimberly, he lives right there.* As if location governed attraction.

"Oh you know he does. He watches you like a hawk when you skim the pool for your folks. There he is, pretending to trim that shrub that has not grown in about six years and looking out the corner of his eye to see if your tits get wet when you lean in too far."

"The pool," I said. "Let's sneak out and take a dip. The kids are fine down in the basement. It's nice and cool down there. We'll take a dip and then we can sleep in my parents' spare room. They have that backup window unit."

She nodded, forgetting to mock Stephen Weber any more. "Good. If we tell the gremlins that they can all camp out down there and stay up as late as they want, it might just work."

"*Fantasy Island* is on next," I reminded her.

"Oh, they will so behave for *Fantasy Island.*"

We tiptoed out the kitchen door, pulling it nearly closed but not all the way. The pool filter was making a soft sucking noise as it churned cool water in a lazy circle. We stripped off our pj's in the dark and stood in the sticky night listening to the cicadas sing. It was a grating, imposing song that never failed to make me think of summertime. "You first," I said, suddenly spooked.

Erin shrugged, climbed the ladder, her white bra and panties glowing almost neon in the purple darkness. If Steve was watching he *would* get an eyeful now. I watched how she moved, so much more sure-footed and self-assured than I could ever be. I had always envied her that, but also felt somehow that her traits were my traits and vice versa. That meant I was confident and self-assured and she was gentle and soft-spoken like me. We were so much alike and so totally different.

Her body made a soft sound parting the water and her splashes mixed with the constant drone of the motor.

"Come on, you big sissy." She laughed. It was a kind laugh, though, no real criticism behind the words.

"I'm gonna kick your ass when I get in there. You are so bossy," I whisper-shouted and climbed the rickety four-step ladder to reach the pool. Here I was all long arms and legs, willowy and tall. Small breasts, flared hips, round ass, small waist. And there she was somewhere in the black water almost straight up and down like a boy, but big breasted. Fine boned. Dark hair to my light. Her breasts were the one thing I truly envied. The boys went berserk over her tits and I would find myself fixated on them. Under her softball uniform, under her gym uniform, and now in there under her wet plain white bra.

"What are you waiting for?" Out of the darkness came her thin but strong hand. She caught hold of me and pulled and then I was falling and making a startled noise like a bird.

We crashed to the water as one, my body pinning hers as the momentum pulled us under. I had a hysterical and wildly comical moment when I wondered if the huge breasts I felt pressed against mine would propel us to the top like flotation devices. I think the thought was a diversion, to divert my startled mind and body from what I was really feeling—a warm peace and a silver-quick arousal at having her smashed under me. We were hipbone to hipbone, waist to waist. Warm skin to warm skin surrounded by water that raised goose bumps and nipples with a chill. We were almost up from the water and my mind was still reeling when she kissed me.

Her lips and tongue tasted like Sir Isaac Lime Otter Pops. When she kissed me deeper the strong taste of chlorinated water invaded but it didn't dull the sweetness.

"People," I started.

"Can't see us," she said to me. She swam to the side, one arm still hooked around me. She had been a lifeguard the past two summers and I could feel that strength in her. The ability to swim while pulling another person along.

"Steve." I laughed when I really just want to kiss her again.

"Is getting a two-for-one deal."

My brain was playing some odd game with itself. Ticking off every time we had been intimate in some way that other girlfriends weren't. The semidrunken kiss at the junior prom when I got upset because we were the only two stag girls there. Except for Carol Presley, who was really there with her cousin Virgil so he didn't count as a date. The back rubs, which had always lingered a bit. But really, nothing overt. Nothing that wasn't a typical exploration. How many girls practiced kissing on each other so they knew what to do when the time came? Only, I wanted to kiss her everywhere. Not just on her green-stained lips and not just so she would know how to kiss Michael Budny when he finally got her alone.

"Stop thinking," she said and kissed me again.

"How did you know I was thinking?" I said, but then I found some of my bravado and stood, pressing her smaller body to the side of the pool with mine. She felt good, warm and soft and eager in the way that she wriggled against me, her tongue dipping farther back in my mouth. She was my best friend and this felt perfectly right.

"Because I know everything you're thinking." The water made it easy; her legs floated up and out and then wrapped around my waist as she clung to me. And I held her effortlessly, thanks to the lapping wetness around us. "You were my prom date." She said it like it was the simplest thing ever.

And then it clicked. I *was* her prom date. I had asked her

why she had said no to Michael Budny. He had clearly asked her, wanted her to go. Her exact words had been, "I'd rather go with you, Kim." Now I understood that she hadn't meant stag, she had meant *with* me. As my date. We had gone as a couple and I hadn't even known. "But I . . ."

"You always were the dense one," she said and her small wet hands roamed my body. "I love you, you idiot. Why do you think I wanted to spend a week back home with a brood of complaining kids rather than go lay on the beach and ogle boys."

Something swelled in my chest then. A good, warm feeling. A sense of rightness. A sense of belonging. All the times I had looked at her pink lips naked of lipstick and wondered what they tasted like had been no big deal. All the times I had watched her get ready for a party and thought how goddamned pretty she was, but not in an envious way, made sense. The lack of envy had always confused me. I figured everyone had confusion as they grew up. I was just getting my wires crossed.

Erin kissed down the side of my neck, licked my collar bone. And then I realized I didn't have my wires crossed. I finally had them straight because all of me—inside and out—was reacting with feelings I had waited and waited for on every date I'd ever gone out on. Feelings that had never ever shown up. Here they were. Want, excitement, a need to touch her more. All of it was blazing out of me like bright white rays of light.

I kissed her hair as her cold, wet hands continued to roam over me. Everywhere at once, now that I knew. I think she was relieved. Over my breasts, my nipples rock hard from the adrenaline and the cool, dark water. Over my waist, dipping down my hips. Feeling her way like she was blind. She wriggled her fingers down the front of my panties and I held my breath, picturing her long thin fingers pushing into my white cotton underwear and finding me. When she did, I bit my tongue to stay silent. Her cold fingers rubbing over my clit triggered hot tears at the corners of my eyes.

"Is this OK, am I OK to do this?" she said against my throat. I nodded and then realized she couldn't see me at all.

"Yes. It's good. Better than good."

We went underwater. Playing in the dark. Kissing and floating in a black nothingness with the background noise of crickets and bugs and distant traffic. I filled my hands with her breasts. Somehow warm even in the chilly water. She was shivering then and so was I. Her nipples poking against my palms and her teeth clacking together so loudly they sounded like novelty teeth. I was the one who said, "Come on, let's go. We'll go up to my parents' bed in the spare room."

"Why do they sleep in the spare room?" she asked and her chattering teeth nearly blocked out her words.

"The spare room has the air-conditioner. And an extra window. It's their summer bed." I was laughing as I pulled her toward the ladder.

The drone of the TV came up from the basement but no other sound. They were all passed out in front of the show. We left wet, streaked footprints on the orange linoleum floor. "Just to get warm," she said, sounding nervous as we climbed the steps to the second floor.

"Just to get warm." I soothed her because I wasn't nervous at all anymore. I wanted her in the big double bed with the plain white sheets and the hum of the window unit blocking out the world. I shucked my panties and my bra in the adjoining bathroom and her dark brown eyes glittered as she watched me. Sitting perched on the edge of the bed, dripping just a little. Rivulets of water streaked her dark hair and a single gem hung from the tip of her nose. I leaned in and kissed it off. "We cannot. I mean, we don't have to." I kissed her nose again and her hands moved to tangle in my hair.

"How do you want something so bad for so long and then get so afraid when it finally happens?" she asked, kissing my eyelids, my cheeks.

"Girls are silly," I said, half whispering. I had yet to flip the AC on. The room was warm, but we were so chilled the stifling heat felt good. "We get all worked up over stuff," I said, softly. Her tongue was soft like wet velvet.

She pulled me back into the bed. It was a mess of lumps and divots. The mattress had been my parents' originally. When they had upgraded, the old mattress had gone into the guest room. Along with the overwashed, well-loved white cotton sheets. So much better than satin or anything fancy. They smelled like lavender and cotton and hot summer sun. "Tell me you love me," she said.

It was easy. I did love her. I always had. Forever and a day. "I love you. I love you in about six different ways."

Her hair was making a wet halo around her head and she cupped my face in her still-shaking hands. "I love you too. I've loved you since you gave me your green crayon in kindergarten."

"That's a long time to keep a secret," I said, laughing. But when I saw the intensity of her gaze, I swallowed the next wave of laughter.

"Yes, it is," she said.

"Yes, it is." I pressed my lips to hers and moved against

her. Just a slow movement of my thighs rubbing over hers. My breast brushing hers. Her neck smelled like the pool water and that gardenia perfume she always wore in the summer. I had always marveled that the bees never swarmed her; she smelled like a giant, sweet flower.

"Touch me," she said into my mouth before her tongue stroked mine more urgently.

I did. I touched her everywhere I could. Her short, damp hair at the place where it curled at the nape of her neck. I traced her earlobes and her cheekbones with my fingertips. She tried to kiss my fingers but I danced them out of the way of her lips to tease her. I touched her long, slender throat and the full, warm swells of her breasts. I put my face against her throat and felt her pulse against my cheek as I pushed my fingers into her panties and found her hot and warm. Her body took me in and she sighed against my ear, arching up into my hand. "I've never been—"

"Me either," I assured her. It seemed important that she know. I'd never been with anyone. Ever. And at that moment, I was so, so happy that I hadn't. So happy that it had never felt right before. That urgency had never egged me on and hormones had never gotten the better of me. But there in the white cotton cocoon with her, I felt like I might fly right off of the earth if Erin weren't holding onto me.

When she came around my fingers, I felt a bizarre and silly sense of pride. That I had made someone other than myself reach an orgasm. When she bit my earlobe in a way that made me see stars, I laughed softly because I knew it had been good. And when she kissed her way down my body, her hot, full lips searing my skin and making me shiver like I was cold again, I was thankful that we had six more nights in the summer bed.

A TRUE AWAKENING

PAM GALLIEN

SANDY STRETCHED HER lean body across the bed to turn off the lamp. The hardwood floor of the master bedroom was illuminated by a beam of light emitted from beneath the bathroom door. "Babe, bring a towel for the wet spot," she said to her lover, chuckling.

Alana bounded from the bathroom with a towel in hand. She threw her naked body across the bed, landing with her lips inches from Sandy's. She held the towel just out of reach. "Do you love me?"

Sandy landed a hard kiss on her lover's lips long enough to free the towel from her grip. "I love you so much that I'm going to sleep on the wet spot."

Alana rolled to her side and tucked her legs under the blankets. "Tell me about your first love."

Sandy laughed as she cuddled next to her partner. "You want to hear about my first lover, after we've just made love?"

Alana rolled on her side, slid her hand down her lover's silky bare skin, searching for her ass. "You can tell a lot about your partner from her first love."

"You're makin' that up." Sandy nuzzled closer in response to the grip on her backside.

"Come on . . . How'd ya meet her?" Alana pressed.

Sandy buried her face in her lover's shoulder and giggled. "I met her in college. . . . We were both dating the same guy."

The curvaceous brunette sat up abruptly. "Now you've got to tell me," she hooted.

Sandy laughed at her partner's curiosity. "Well . . . I was taking summer classes at the time and I was going steady with this guy, Doug. It all started when he cancelled a date with me at the last minute. It was his last mistake." Sandy huffed at the memory.

◆

SANDY MALONE DROPPED her butt on the edge of her dormitory bed as the phone landed in its cradle. She couldn't deny her disappointment at Doug's last-minute cancellation. Saturday night was the one night a week her schedule was free of studies, work, or classes. By now, her girlfriends would certainly have plans of their own, which meant she would be flying solo on date night.

It was the summer of her sophomore year. She had been dating Doug O'Hanian since the second semester of her freshman year at UCF. He was the captain of the soccer team, a real hunk, and a lucky catch. She knew very well he could have any girl on campus, but he had picked her. Attractive, popular guys had always been drawn to Sandy. She knew on some level that it was their ego that drew them to her aloofness. It was not a conceit, as much as a disconnect that she possessed. In the mirror, Sandy only saw an average-looking girl with no significant attributes. Others could see an attractive, soft-spoken young woman with a quiet confidence.

In frustration, she flopped back on her bed to stare at the ceiling. Sandy mulled over her relationship with Doug. She wasn't even sure she would call it a *relationship*. There were no strong feelings between them. She consented to sex because that's what girls did, not because she enjoyed it. In fact, she found it embarrassing, clumsy, and sometimes repulsive. She had always picked her boyfriends for parental approval and she never truly bonded with any of them. She knew Doug was no different from the others.

She pulled herself up, grabbed a button-up sweater from her footlocker, and headed for the campus cafeteria. Dressed in a sleeveless green blouse with pleated white shorts that flaunted her shapely arms and legs, she knew she looked too good to sit alone in her dorm. Her shaggy, strawberry blonde hair swung softly about her shoulders. Silver hoop earrings dangling from her earlobes peeked through her mane. She usually drew a fair amount of admiring looks, but she never seemed to notice.

The night was too beautiful to sit around and sulk. She decided to grab a bite to eat, check out a movie at the cinema, then call it a night. The late-August breeze carried a hint of ocean salt on it. A retired sun had left a purple hue to the west and a swath of twinkling stars to the east. The evening had a dreamlike quality.

Truth be known, Sandy enjoyed her alone time. She slung her sweater over her shoulder as she strolled across campus, breathing in nature's bliss. A group of fraternity boys interrupted the evening's serenity with hoots and howls as they sped by in a souped-up car. Cuddling couples whispered by her on both sides of the street. She had not even noticed Doug with another girl until they were upon her. He stopped in his tracks, yanking his date to an unexpected halt. Sandy took notice of the girl immediately without looking directly at her. Her imploring eyes sought an explanation, but none came.

Doug tried to contain the situation. "Hey, Sandy . . . uh," he stammered slightly. "Michelle . . . Sandy . . . Sandy . . . Michelle."

Sandy felt the yellow hue of the streetlamps only added to the surrealism of his cavalier introduction. Muddled thoughts of embarrassment, rage, and even physical assault flashed through her mind. Sandy's eyes drifted to the dark-haired beauty standing beside her boyfriend. She caught her first glimpse of Michelle's satin black mane reflecting the streetlight like a moonbeam. Michelle assessed the situation with a reluctant scan of Sandy's face. The dark-haired beauty slowly released Doug's hand as her eyes shifted from quizzical to wounded. Sandy's heart liquefied. For the first time in her life, she felt an instant connection with another human being. She wanted to reach out and touch this stranger's face, so full of emotion. This doleful beauty tortured her heart. *We must be stopping traffic. God, she's beautiful!* Sandy cautiously extended her hand to Michelle. Michelle accepted. The two women stood face-to-face with their hands locked in a gentle embrace.

Michelle slowly withdrew her fragile, warm fingers with a perplexed look. "Nice to meet you," she said, her voice barely escaping her lips.

Her murmur was soft and velvety to Sandy's ears.

"Nice to meet you too," Sandy returned in a whisper. It was at that moment she lost her heart to another woman. Sandy turned an angry eye on Doug. "Don't bother calling me again."

She turned and left them standing in the yellow spotlight of the streetlamp.

◆

"OUCH! I BET his ears were ringing for days," Alana hooted. "What'd Michelle do?"

"Well . . . I found out from my so-called friends that her name was Michelle Greer, and Doug had been dating her behind my back for some time. I also found out that she dumped him that night too."

"Good for her!" Alana cheered.

"Yeah!" Sandy smiled, as she rolled onto her back. "Anyway, I couldn't get her out of my mind. I kept picturing her eyes and hair under that streetlight. I became obsessed. I found out what her major was. I learned she was a sorority girl and found her sorority house. For months, I tried like hell for that chance meeting. My inability to find her just made it worse. I had never felt such longing, or such a need and desire to be with someone. God, it hurt sooo gooood." Sandy sighed. "I wasn't sure what I'd do when I ran into her. I don't even think sex was a notion . . . I just needed to be around her . . . near her . . . to see and talk to her." Sandy sat quietly for a moment, caught in the nostalgia. "I know I had never felt such intensity before then."

"So how'd ya finally run into her?" Alana was eager to hear the rest of the love story.

"I spent more time at the library and student cafeteria. I'd walk past her sorority house whenever possible. I finally caught a glimpse of her one night about a month after our introduction. She was in a car with some guy. They appeared to be on a date. It broke my heart. That was the first time I realized that I wanted more than just to be with her. I started fantasizing about her body. I'd see her standing under the same streetlamp, naked and vulnerable. I made love to her, mentally, in every conceivable place and way. . . . Whew! That was the best sex I ever had," Sandy snorted.

Alana nuzzled closer to Sandy and slid a hand between her legs. "OK, now you're turning me on," she purred.

Caught up in the memory, Sandy kissed the tip of her partner's nose and continued, "I finally did run into her. She didn't recognize me at first. I seemed familiar but it took a minute for her to place me. I was a little disappointed. I had hoped our first meeting had been as profound for her, but I didn't see that in her eyes."

"Oh that's so sad," consoled the sultry brunette beside her.

The smirk on Sandy's face said "easy come, easy go" even though the memory of that first love still left her forlorn.

◆

IT WAS MID-FEBRUARY and fairly brisk for Florida. Sandy could barely hear the click of her heels over the blowing winds. Unable to bear the chill any longer, she broke into a trot about thirty feet from the front door of the Coffee Hut, a local student hangout. She was hoping to chase the blues away with a cappuccino. It had been two days since she vowed to put Michelle behind her. She had pretty much given up on the two of them ever crossing paths. She had even accepted a date with a guy in her physics class, in a conscious effort to get her life back on track.

She entered the shop and set the bell above the door in motion. A couple in a back booth turned their heads in passing interest. Sandy skirted by a coed, sitting alone at a table with her nose buried in a book.

The girl behind the counter dog-eared the page she was on before laying down her paperback to greet Sandy. "What can I get ya?"

Sandy perused the billboard menu behind the counter. "I'll have a family-sized mocha cappuccino, soy creamer, a dash of nutmeg, and a cinnamon stick, please . . . Oh, extra cream and sugar too."

"Cream and sugar's on the counter against the wall." Her tone indicated that Sandy was not the first customer to make this egregious request.

Sandy coughed "*bitch*" under her breath as she grabbed her order and headed for the condiment counter. *Jesus, girl, if you'd spend less time reading your romance novels and a little more time doing your job, this counter might not look like the bottom of a Dumpster.* As she gingerly picked sugar packets from the sticky counter, her eyes scanned the shop looking for a comfortable, quiet corner. Her heart dragged a beat before taking off in a gallop when she caught sight of Michelle's head buried in a textbook. For a fleeting moment she considered fleeing before she was noticed. *Jesus, she'll know as soon as she lays eyes on me that she's all I think about! It's written all over this stupid face!*

Feeling a gaze upon her, Michelle lifted her head. Her eyes met Sandy's with that familiar perplexity Sandy had engraved in her memory. Sandy managed to choke on a clumsy hello. Michelle returned an affable smile before her eyes drifted back to her book. That very moment, Sandy could feel her heart wither. Like a slab of chiseled granite, she remained breathless, cold, and unmovable.

Suddenly, Michelle's chin bobbed up. "I know you!"

As if the Victrola had received a surge of electricity, Sandy blurted enthusiastically, "I should hope so. I saved you from going out with one of the biggest assholes on campus." Beaming with the biggest smile to ever paint her face, she immediately pulled up a chair at the table.

"Yeah, I guess I do owe you." Michelle grinned back with the same shy smile Sandy had envisioned countless times.

The angelic face across the table released joyous butterflies in Sandy's stomach. She extended a hand. "Sandy."

Michelle softly grasped the offered hand. "Michelle."

"So what're you reading?" Sandy inquired.

Michelle closed the book, hiked her feet on a neighboring chair, and responded, "Oh. I'm just trying to catch up on my government class. But I was looking for an excuse to put it down."

◆

SANDY KISSED HER partner on the forehead. "So that's it. We talked until the place closed."

Alana abruptly sat up in the bed. "That's it?"

"Yeah that's how we met."

"Where're the details?" she prodded.

"Ha! You want the details?"

"Come on, girl. How do you go from dating the same guy, to a chance encounter, to lovers?" the sultry brunette demanded.

"OK, OK!" Sandy opened her arm, allowing a cove for her lover to nestle in. Alana slid her warm silky skin against her lover's body and cuddled in her arms.

Sandy continued, "I didn't exactly come out and tell her how I felt. But I know my body language and shameless flirting got the message across. To my amazement, she didn't bolt in the opposite direction. She seemed to enjoy my attraction to her. After a month of wooing her, I invited her over to watch a movie and drink a few beers."

◆

SANDY FLUFFED THE throw pillows her mother had sent for Christmas then tossed them on the bed. She lit some candles on the desk before killing the overhead light. The lamp across the room blended with the flickering candles for a soft, romantic glow. She popped a Sade tape in the boombox and lowered the volume for soft background music. Hearing a tap at the door, she quickly darted to the mirror for one last primping. She cleaned the mascara from the corners of her eyes, took two deep breaths, then opened the door.

Michelle held out a six-pack of cheap beer. "I hope you have a fridge. Or we're gonna have to shotgun these beers."

Sandy motioned her in, snapping one beer from the plastic ring as Michelle skirted by. "The fridge is in the corner. The pizza's on the way. Hope you like vegetarian."

Michelle shoved the remaining beers into the half-size icebox. "I like your room. Where's your roommate?"

"She's gone home for the weekend. So if you get too wasted you can use her bed tonight."

"Cool. So what did ya get for movies?"

Sandy threw herself across the bed and grabbed the DVDs off the desk. "I got two. I didn't know what you'd like. We got action and we got sex."

"Sex!" Michelle laughed.

There was an abrupt rap on the door. "Pizza!"

Sandy sprang from the bed. "I got it."

Michelle popped open a beer, slid off her leather jacket,

and tossed it on the spare bed. A gray, loose-knit sweater hung on her bra-less bosom, exposing the outline of erect nipples. Sandy closed the door, caught a glimpse of Michelle's buoyant breasts, and stumbled on her way to the desk. Michelle leapt from the bed to save the pizza. Her full mammaries gently swayed beneath the mohair sweater.

"Jeez. Careful."

"Ah . . . thanks . . . ahh . . . I got it," Sandy stammered.

"You're not the type that gets trashed off one beer, are you?"

"Nooo. I'm fine. I just tripped . . . on the rug." Sandy placed the box on the desktop. They both fell silent for an awkward moment.

Michelle looked into Sandy's eyes, tilted her head, and smiled. "Are you hungry?"

Sandy felt paralyzed by the heat Michelle generated with her gaze. She blushed and stammered, "Yeah . . . sure." She backed away, feeling suddenly bashful and claustrophobic. Grabbing the movie from its jacket, she shoved it into the machine. As an afterthought, she headed across the room to douse the light. The light from the television illuminated the dorm with white-gray shadows. "Too dark?"

Michelle propped herself up at the head of the bed. "No, that's perfect."

Sandy snatched herself a piece of pie and slid into the spot left for her. Michelle squirmed on the single bed trying to make more room for Sandy. "I feel funny using your roommate's bed without asking."

"This is fine." Sandy's heart palpitated. "You OK?" Michelle made one last squirm. "Sure, I'm comfortable."

The two sat side by side with their legs extended the length of the bed. The movie opened with an ample-breasted blonde on all fours and a muscular man furiously slamming himself into her buttocks. Sandy's face flushed. She swallowed hard on the shock.

"Jeezus! Is this X-rated?" Michelle gasped.

"I don't think so? It's supposed to be an erotic murder mystery."

They froze with embarrassment as the couple on screen climaxed in a screaming frenzy. Sandy felt Michelle's leg twitch. Her own breathing receded to a shallow wisp. Ten minutes of dialogue followed, none of which Sandy absorbed. She had barely recovered from the last sex scene when another couple flashed on the screen. These two appeared in an elevator. A shirtless muscular stud in snug jeans forcefully lifted a brunette's skirt as she frantically tugged at his zipper. Sandy felt as though the temperature in the room had shot up ten degrees. She was about to suggest the other movie when Michelle placed a hand on her thigh. Sandy felt her heart punch through her chest.

"Does that bother you?" Michelle whispered.

"No . . . it . . . feels nice," Sandy stammered in a gravelly voice.

Neither girl moved. On the screen, the elevator shot symbolically to the top of the high-rise. Michelle gently dug her nails into Sandy's thigh and a circus of somersaults enveloped Sandy's stomach. *Oh God, I can't breathe.* Sandy closed her eyes as she pressed her head against the wall. Michelle's hand slowly ran up and down the length of Sandy's thigh, brushing over Sandy's mound, before locking onto her crotch. They both turned their heads, searching for lips, bumping teeth as they hastily lowered their bodies on the bed. Sandy briefly tasted blood before Michelle sucked it away. Lifting the knitted sweater, she touched the soft flesh of Michelle's full breasts. She lowered her head and locked her lips on a quarter-sized nipple. She sucked, licked, and nibbled until Michelle's moans drowned out the television. Like a whirlwind, outerwear began to fly across the room; the undergarments quickly followed until both women lay bare and sweaty, locked in a love knot.

Sandy's stomach rolled as her fingers twirled in Michelle's wetness, teasing softly. She steadily worked her way down the length of Michelle's body before running her tongue between her thighs, now drenched with excitement. Methodically, she jutted her tongue over and around Michelle's fold. Michelle gripped the sheets in her fists and arched her back. Her hips thrashed, begging for more. Sandy teased without mercy, gently licking then engulfing Michelle's pinkness with her mouth. Michelle's body locked hard with a domino of eruptions. Sandy needed to feel closer. She raised Michelle's leg then positioned her hips until they melded their drenched warmth. They gently rotated their pubic bones in unison, sliding back and forth, feeling each other's satiny heat. Sandy pinched and kneaded Michelle's rosy nipples as the gyrations increased in tempo. Their moans grew louder and louder until they climaxed in unison. Sandy slumped on top of Michelle. Misty with perspiration, they kissed passionately.

◆

ALANA MURMURED, "SO when was the last time you spoke to her?"

"We lost touch after college. Last I heard she was married and living outside of Boston, with a baby on the way," Sandy whispered in Alana's ear.

"Was that the only time you made love?" Alana pressed.

Sandy chuckled at her partner's persistence. "No, we

dated on the sly for two years. The entire time she continued to date guys. Like a fool, I hung on to every morsel of attention she gave me."

Alana purred. "Her loss, my gain . . . baby."

Sandy ran her hand down the shapely curves of her girlfriend's body to the small of her back. She knew that Michelle had been a true awakening, but Alana was a true love. She pulled the love of her life closer. "She was a flash in the pan, sweetie. You're a keeper." She smiled in the dark.

Alana smiled back as she drifted off to sleep. "That's right, baby. . . . I'm for keeps."

OPENING NIGHT

CHARLOTTE DARE

HER SPIKY BLACK hair shone purple under the stage lights, and her movements were as graceful as a dancer's. The night of auditions for Neil Simon's *Rumors*, Mari delivered the lines for Chris in a throaty drawl that would've made Kathleen Turner jealous. I couldn't peel my eyes off of her. The newest member of the Shoreline Players had a stage presence sure to steal every scene.

Throughout our six-week rehearsal schedule, I found myself shadowing Mari at every opportunity, chalking it up to professional admiration. In my early twenties, community theater was more than a creative outlet. It was an escape from myself—the chance to be someone else under the noble disguise of artistic expression. I may have been fooling myself, but looking back, Mari had me pegged from our first read-through.

"We have a great cast," she said as we left the theater. "You're going to make a wonderful Cassie."

"Thanks," I said, "but I can't picture myself as the perky newlywed type. Of course, I don't tell my boyfriend that."

She nodded with mild amusement. "He must enjoy watching you perform."

"Eh," I began, tilting my hand from side to side. "But

after sitting through *Macbeth* and *A Winter's Tale,* he said he'll be glad to see me in a play he can understand."

She smirked. "He's not a fan of high art?"

"Sadly, no," I said. "Unless it involves watching guys try to get a ball from one place to another, Jason's not interested. But he does do a good job faking it."

Mari chuckled as she twirled her car keys. "How does he feel about you spending so much time at rehearsals?"

"Not crazy about the idea. He doesn't come right out and say it, but he gives plenty of subtle clues." Before I knew it, Mari had walked me to my car under an orangey streetlight.

"Well, I wouldn't let anyone persuade you off the stage. From what I've seen, you're very talented." Her smile was forceful and her eyes lingered on mine for an uncomfortably long time.

"Thanks." I felt my face flush. When she walked off to her car, I just stood there watching her. For the first time in years, I hadn't had to justify refusing to give up the stage to meet someone else's emotional needs.

I followed the taillights of Mari's Prius for about two miles until she took a right at a stop sign and disappeared into the night. For a split second, I actually thought of following to see where she lived. I should've known right then that something was happening, but the blinders were still securely in place.

✦

BY THE END of the first week of rehearsals, I was getting more butterflies in my stomach waiting for Mari to walk in than I did thinking about opening night.

"How's it going, Cassie?" she whispered as she plunked down in the chair I'd saved for her by throwing my leg across it.

"Hiya Chris." I smiled like a fool as I pretended to listen to the director drone on.

"Does anybody have any questions before we block the last scene in Act One?" he asked. "I know we're moving fast, but I want to start running the show as soon as possible."

"He does know we're not in the running for a Tony, doesn't he?" Mari drawled. I stifled a laugh.

Later, as Mari and I stood in the wings waiting for our respective cues, I had a heightened sense of her presence—the whisper of her deep breathing and the fruity smell of her hair gel as she leaned toward me and stretched—things I'd never noticed about anyone else I'd done a show with.

She crunched on a Granny Smith apple she'd fished out of her bag as she wobbled in her character shoes. "These damn things never fit right. I have to get a new pair." She tossed the core in the garbage and clutched at my shoulder, leaning practically all of her weight on me. "Don't mind me. I think I have a pebble in here."

I didn't mind at all. In fact, I relished the sensation of the pressure from her hand as she balanced herself on one foot.

"There, that's better," she said. "Hey, are you going to the Cantina tonight for drinks?"

I hadn't planned to. Jason wanted me to meet him for coffee after rehearsal. "Are you?" I asked.

She raised an eyebrow at the absurdity of the question. "I teach kindergarten, so if I don't do happy hour with the faculty on Fridays, then you better believe I'm going out with the cast after rehearsal. Besides, the Cantina has the most extraordinary veggie nachos. We can take one car if you'd like to save some gas."

I thought about Jason's reaction and smiled in spite of myself. "Who doesn't want to save gas?"

"Since I have the hybrid, I'll drive," she said and charged into her scene with fluid timing.

◆

BY AROUND TEN o'clock, six of us from the cast and crew had stuffed ourselves into a corner booth at the Cantina and were having a raucous time laughing at each other's scene flubs and slip-ups earlier in the evening. I was shoulder to shoulder with Mari, savoring every sensuous experience from the tangy taste of the appetizers and drinks to the tickle of her firm arm brushing against mine to the clean scent of her patchouli oil. As an added bonus, Mari was a laugh-leaner—every time she laughed, she would lean into the person who'd amused her. The moment I realized this, I practically turned into a stand-up comedienne.

"You're a riot, Kim," she cooed after composing herself enough to take a sip of her raspberry margarita. "It's true. You never realize how many words in the English language have *S* in them until you have a conversation with a person who lisps."

She giggled again, and just as I was in the midst of secretly congratulating myself, my cell phone sang with "The Name of the Game" from the *Mamma Mia* soundtrack. I looked down and was horrified to see it was Jason calling. How could I have forgotten to call and tell him I wasn't going to meet him for coffee?

"I have to take this," I said with a dour expression. I hurried into the hall near the bathrooms. "Hello?" I answered as if I had no idea what the call was about.

"Where the hell are you?" he bellowed. "I waited twenty minutes at the coffeehouse and now I'm at an empty theater."

"I'm at the Cantina. I'm sorry. We were in such a rush I forgot to call you."

"Nice. So now you're blowing me off to hang out with the people you just spent all night with?" Suddenly, his clues weren't so subtle. "That's bullshit."

"Jason, I didn't mean to blow you off. Why don't you come down here now and join us?" As soon as it came out, I hoped he wouldn't say yes.

He was still steaming. "I mean is this how it's going to be with this group?"

"Jason, you know part of the experience is hanging out and unwinding afterwards. It's nothing against you. You said you understood about this kind of stuff."

"I do, but we had plans. I can't friggin' believe you forgot to call me."

He sounded so hurt, and as much as I wanted to get back to the table, I couldn't help feeling guilty. "Jason, I'm sorry."

"How much longer are you going to be down there?"

"An hour or so. Maybe less."

"Forget it. I'll just see you tomorrow night. We *are* still on for our anniversary dinner tomorrow night, aren't we?"

"Definitely. Good night." The abruptness of my good-bye did little to corroborate my contrition. I rushed back to the table and slid in next to Mari.

"You're not in trouble, are you?" she asked. The way she said it sounded more like a dare than an expression of concern.

"Of course not. I just reminded him this is what the cast does on Friday nights during the show—isn't it?"

"I'd say so with this crew." She looked at me with eyes that brimmed with sensitivity. She understood something about me, although I had no idea what. I didn't know what to say at that moment, but I couldn't look away from her. "You are allowed to have a good time on your own, Kim." She patted my leg just above the knee and took another sip of her margarita.

◆

AS THE WEEKS blazed on, I regularly caught myself thinking about Mari. At work, at home, spending time with Jason, it didn't matter—some random thought about her would sneak into my consciousness and sweep me away. The night of our anniversary, the last time Jason made love to me, I couldn't keep my mind from wandering. When he kissed me, I imagined it was Mari's lips trailing down my neck. When he penetrated me, it was with Mari's fingers. I actually orgasmed that night, but it wasn't Jason who'd brought me there. I left his place in the morning feeling dirty, trying to convince myself that those thoughts didn't mean anything. It had to be because I was spending so much time with Mari at rehearsal.

◆

THE SUNDAY BEFORE we opened, I called and asked her if she could run lines with me that night—not an unusual request save for the fact that I knew my lines cold. I was still steeped in vigorous denial, but once again, Mari was one step ahead of me.

After we'd run through the last scene, she plopped down on her sofa and raked a hand through her hair. "See? I told you there's nothing to worry about."

I collapsed in a cushy chair across from her. "Well, in live theater there's no such thing as too 'prepared.'"

"That's why I love performing with you. You have such respect for your craft." She grinned and crossed her legs on the coffee table, folding her arms behind her head. "So, you wanna tell me the real reason you're here? Does it have to do with Jason?"

Just when I thought I could relax. Finally, my hands weren't shaking and I wasn't pulverizing breath mints to keep my mouth hydrated anymore. Now this. "What do you mean," I stammered. "I'm nervous about the show."

"You're nervous about something, but I doubt it's the show. You haven't forgotten a line in rehearsal yet. Shit, you even know everyone else's."

I sighed and desperately tried to climb out of the hole I'd unwittingly dug. "All right," I lied. "It is about Jason." I conjured a pained facade.

"What's the matter?" Her tone was so warm and comforting; I just wanted to crawl into her lap.

"We're not getting along like we used to," I said.

"Is it you or him?"

"I don't know. We're fighting all the time, especially since I started the show."

"It's probably because he's feeling left out and missing you, that's all," she said. When I looked up from absently studying my cuticles, she was staring over at me with a seductive smile. "I can't really blame him."

I giggled but looked down again. The conversation was opening doors I wasn't prepared to move through. "But there's nothing wrong with him. He's a good guy. It must be me."

"Maybe it is you. You probably need some time to figure out what you want."

"What I want?"

She shifted her position Indian-style on the sofa, her tanned toes peeking out from under her knees. "Maybe you don't want what it is you think you want."

"What do you mean?" I said, flustered. "Like maybe I want a guy with blond hair or a different job? I'm not sure what—"

"Maybe not a guy at all." She threw it out there as casually as if we were ordering Chinese food.

"I don't think so," I said with an anxious chuckle.

Mari smiled and shrugged. "It's not the end of the world if it's true."

"I know that. I'm cool with gay people. I have gay friends."

"Present company included I hope." Another flirty smile.

Ripples of nerves shot through my stomach. "I should get going now. I have to get up for work in six hours."

She draped her hand around my shoulder as she walked me to the door. "Look, I wouldn't worry about anything, Kim. I'm sure things will be fine with you and Jason after the show closes."

I stopped at the front door and gazed into her golden-flecked eyes. "Thanks."

"Any time." She rubbed the side of my shoulder. "Now relax. And think about everything I said—just think about it."

As I walked down the stone steps, I wasn't sure which of Mari's parting words left me feeling so unraveled—that I might be gay or that things would indeed be fine with Jason again.

◆

OPENING NIGHT WAS electric. The entire cast's energy and timing were spot on, and for once, I delivered a near-flawless performance. Mari hosted the opening-night celebration after the show, cramming all of us into her quaint Cape on the beach. Although I enjoyed the company of everyone, my attention belonged solely to Mari. It was after one a.m. when the last guest left—last except me, that is.

"Are you sure you're all right to drive home?" Mari asked as I lingered at the front door.

"I had one wine cooler two hours ago," I replied.

"I'll take that as a 'yes,'" she said. "That's too bad. Tomorrow's going to be a gorgeous day to relax out on the beach." She turned and glanced out her French doors at the moonlight bobbing on the choppy water.

Was she trying to get me to stay over? "It is kind of late and I do live almost an hour away," I said.

She smiled knowingly. "I love it when the tide comes in this time of night. Would you like to look out at the water?"

"Sure."

We leaned over the porch railing together, resting on our elbows, listening to the waves roll onto her slip of private beach.

"Wow," I gushed. "It must be amazing to fall asleep to this sound every night."

"It makes everything more amazing." As she studied my face, her scent floated over me on the breeze.

She smelled delicious and by now it was impossible to rationalize the way she was making me feel. She leaned in and gently kissed me. *I should protest, shouldn't I? Back away or something.* But I didn't want to. She cupped my cheek in her hand and kissed me again—slow, sensual kisses that were warm and wet and unlike anything I'd ever felt. I tingled all over as she wrapped her arms around my neck and pulled me to her, slowly exploring my mouth with her tongue.

"You're so beautiful, Kim," she breathed. She stroked my arms with her painted fingernails, giving me chills in the warm night air. "I'd love to make love to you," she whispered and kissed my neck softly.

"I've never been with a woman before," I said as my knees buckled from the pleasure of her touch.

"I know, honey," she said, nibbling my earlobe.

Confused, nervous, and aroused beyond my wildest dreams, I wanted to hop over the railing and run away. "But I don't know what to do."

A low, sensual giggle vibrated in my ear. "You will when I'm through with you." She led me in through the French doors, leaving them wide open. When she switched off the living room lamp, the flickering votives on the mantel and the full moon peering in through the open doors illuminated our faces.

We stopped at her oversized sofa and kissed some more. Her hands spread out over my body, caressing my arms and lower back under my shirt. I dared to slide my hands down to her ass and squeezed.

"Oh, Kim," she breathed.

I felt a surge between my legs like I'd never known. I was wet and throbbing and terrified. I'd never felt this with Jason or any other boyfriend. I didn't know what it all meant, but I knew I didn't want Mari to stop.

She pulled her own shirt off and then mine and lowered me onto her plush sofa. Her warm stomach felt so good against my skin as she licked my neck and exhaled in my ear. She unhooked my bra and dove onto my hard nipples, sucking one while rubbing the other. I wanted so badly to feel her fingers down there, to guide her hand onto me, but inhibition held me captive. So I lay there craving her as she slowly drove me insane with a marathon of erotic play.

When the last of our clothes finally came off, she kissed my stomach as she made her way down my body. The smell of the beach drifted in with the night breeze while Mari's tongue tickled my thighs. I clutched the sofa cushions at the warmth of her breath and smoothness of her fingertips fondling the backs of my legs. Before I knew it, her firm tongue was on my clit. She took her time whirling around, teasing me to the point where I practically begged her to make me come. Finally, she penetrated me, thrusting in and out, riveting my body with intense pulses of pleasure.

Normally quiet during sex, I heard myself gasping and groaning, calling out Mari's name. I gripped the sofa cushions harder as my climax began rising, carrying me away to ecstasy. As I got louder, Mari grabbed my hips tightly and drilled her tongue into me until I came harder than I'd ever imagined. "Holy shit," I gasped as my legs shuddered.

She snuggled up to me while I caught my breath. "Did you like that?" she asked, and kissed my cheeks and nose.

"You were right. Everything's better by the shore."

After a few moments of nuzzling, Mari took my hand and placed it on her pussy. She was silky and wet, and she started slowly moving my fingers up and down, letting me take control gradually. She moaned in my ear and pumped away in time with the rhythm of my hand as she began climaxing. It was so hot watching her orgasm! She'd aroused me all over again.

It was somewhere around four a.m. by the time we were both satiated enough to fall asleep entwined in her Egyptian cotton sheets.

♦

THE NEXT MORNING I sat on the warped wood of Mari's back porch watching the seagulls swoop down on the rocky shore at low tide.

"What are you doing up so early? It's only ten after seven," Mari said at the back door. When I didn't answer, she padded outside in her bare feet and sat down next to me. "Why are you crying?"

"I don't know," I said, wiping my cheek with the side of my hand.

She shaded her eyes from the bright morning sun. "Do you feel weird about last night?"

"No, last night was incredible. I think that's what's making me feel weird."

She gently rubbed my back. "Some people think coming out to the world takes guts." She shook her head with certainty. "Coming out to yourself takes more guts than anything."

"So am I a lesbian?" I asked, choking back my jumbled emotions.

Mari squeezed my shoulder. "I can't answer that for you, honey. But based on your responses last night, I'd say you're at least halfway there."

I laughed through a sob. "How do I find out for sure?"

"You have to be honest with yourself. It'll be easier to figure out if you can do that."

"I care about Jason, but I don't feel for him what I feel for you. I've never felt that way about any guy I've dated."

She grinned. "What do you feel for me?"

I sighed and just started babbling. "I don't know. I think about you all the time, and when I know I'm going to see you, I get all jittery. I hate saying good night, and at rehearsal, I hate it when you talk to other people. And when we're not at rehearsal, I try to think up excuses to call you. And sometimes when I look at you—I forget to breathe." I clammed up when I finally noticed the astonished look on Mari's face. "I'm in love with you, aren't I?"

"It would appear that way." She sighed and leaned forward, staring pensively out across the water.

"What's the matter?" I said, sensing her distance.

"I wasn't very responsible last night," she said, clasping her fingers together.

Her tone was disquieting. "What do you mean?"

"I knew you were attracted to me, but, god, I never thought you could be in love with me. I just figured it was an experience we'd both enjoy."

I cleared my throat bravely. "And you don't have those feelings for me."

"I didn't say that. The thing is I'm eleven years older than you. I've been out forever, and I'm comfortable with who I am and what I want."

I licked the last tear from my lip and felt my ears getting hot. "So then you used me?"

"No, of course I didn't. Frankly, I don't want to be used by you. I'd rather not be the test case that either sends you back the other way or serves as a spring board for your new life as a socially active lesbian. I really could fall for you, Kim, but I know the timing isn't right for us."

"How could you be so sure?"

She stood up and loomed over me, full of arrogance. "Because I know how these things work; I've seen it before. Some older, supposedly wiser woman gets all worked up over an ingénue she leads to her sexual awakening, only to get dumped when the little dykling flies off to discover what treasures the exotic and enticing lesbian world has to offer."

I said nothing for a moment, challenging her with a cold, penetrating stare. "Fine, Mari. I get it. We had our one night of passion. You fucked me so good I could never go back to guys even if I wanted to. So now what? When the show closes, we just go our separate ways?"

"We'll have to play it by ear," she said.

I hugged my knees and fumed silently.

"Kim, we'd be making a huge mistake jumping into something."

"Maybe I should just stay with Jason," I said.

"And you'd be cheating two people with that decision," she said. She trudged back inside and stopped at the screen door. "Make that three."

✦

WE BARELY SURVIVED the three-week run of *Rumors,* thanks to my stubborn lovesick melodrama. When I wasn't shooting Mari evil glances across the wings, I was wrenching my arm from her grip backstage whenever she tried to draw me into a civilized conversation. But in the end, Mari was right. I needed time—time to part ways with Jason, to reconcile my own feelings, and begin the coming out process, all of which I needed to do on my own.

Mari's right about a lot of things and never one to gloat. Yet for some reason she's enjoyed reminding me of our *Rumors* days on every anniversary for the past five years.

TOUR OF DUTY

T. LEE

MY THREE-YEAR HITCH in the armed forces was over. I was now on a Greyhound headed for home after joining the military fresh out of high school. Leaving for boot camp just two weeks after graduation had been a hard thing to do. I'd joined the military for more reasons than I had reasons to stay. While I was away, I'd thought of the last few days I spent at home when things got tough. The last person I'd seen before I got on that plane to leave was Melissa. She would have been the biggest reason I'd had to stay. I felt bad for leaving her when I saw her standing there in the airport, crying, but I just had to find myself. We'd been lovers since we were sophomores in high school. We kept our forbidden love hidden from the people in that school and that small town. That was only because nobody would have accepted us. To understand the concept of two women in love with each other would have been difficult for the people in that little farm town. Melissa and I figured it was just better to keep our passionate love affair a secret. The first two years I'd been gone on my leave we'd written sensual love letters to one another. I used to sit and read them again and again when I found myself missing her so. All of them I had memorized and underlined in red—every single *I love you* she had written in her elegant handwriting. Somewhere in the beginning of the third year our writing letters to one another tapered off and eventually stopped. With that fact in my mind, I couldn't help wondering if this adventure home would reunite us. I also wondered if while I was away she had thought about me as often as I did her and if she still lived in that big white house at the end of Dilly Lane. If she would even know I was coming home. From the never-ending gossip that circled the town, I'm sure she did.

The bus depot came into view as the bus rounded the corner of Central and Third. I was surprised to see that little farm town had grown somewhat since I'd been gone. There was now a Pizza Hut in the building I knew as the Old Feed and Seed. In fact, the business district of downtown had grown quite a bit. Although I was kind of relieved to see some things were still familiar to me. That the entire town hadn't changed. The Bootleg Tavern was still there across the street from the bus depot and Grammy and Gramps Hardware was still in the building beside it.

Catching my eye as I stepped off the bus was the reflection of myself in the window of the bus depot. It got me to thinking for a moment on how much I'd changed too since I'd been in that small town. I'd lost a few pounds and filled out quite nicely thanks to the armed forces. The scrawny zit-faced teenager I was when I left had changed a lot. My complexion had cleared up and I actually had a noticeable bust line. I looked slender and maybe a little taller in my dress uniform. The long brown flowing hair I used to have was now cut short and neat just above my collar line. My sweet Melissa, my lover, always adored my long hair and used to run her fingers through it.

Figuring now I was a grown woman of twenty-one years old, I'd go inside the Bootleg Tavern to relax a bit and gather my thoughts over a beer or two. I went in and sat down at a little table by the jukebox. All the people in there seemed to be quiet and stayed to themselves. There were people bellied up to a big oak bar drinking and laughing amongst themselves, while others sat at little tables scattered around the dimly lit, cigarette smoke–filled room. As I was looking about the room, a familiar face appeared from around the side of a video poker machine. It was a warm, friendly face I remembered from my high school days. It was Mr. Miller, the math teacher. His beard, somewhat grayer than I remembered and his face a little more round and plump from a few extra pounds he had gained. He came over, gave me a firm handshake, and said, "Little Donna Jones, your brother told me you were coming home."

My brother, Travis, was five years younger than I and was probably taking Mr. Miller's math class. "Mr. Miller," I replied as I shook his hand. Just before he sat down at the table I then asked, "So how have you been?"

He replied, "There is no need to call me Mr. Miller now that you're all grown up. You can call me by my first name, Robert." He sat down in the chair across the little table from me then he motioned to the bartender to bring us over a couple beers. We sat there talking and carrying on for about an hour or so before he had to be on his way home. He bought me another beer before he left and gave me a light pat on my shoulder, telling me not to be such a stranger and to stop by his house to visit him and his wife sometime. As I sat there drinking my beer, listening to the soft country music spill out of that old jukebox, my mind pondered what my plans for the evening to come would be.

I thought to myself, I'll go rent a motel room then get out of my dress uniform, shower, and just relax a little more before calling mom and dad.

I was well into my third beer when suddenly my nose caught an old familiar scent. Pausing for a moment and thinking about it, I knew that smell quite well. It was Melissa's perfume. I would sit and smell its florescence on the letters I received from her while I was away. It would remind me of the many nights we had spent together when we loved each other. My heart started pounding and about jumped out of my chest. I could feel all the blood in my body begin to rush to my face as I stood and turned around. My eyes welled up with tears and must have been as big as fifty-cent pieces when I saw that beautiful girl with long red hair I'd loved so long ago. I was trapped in the moment, unsure of exactly what to do. I felt like yelling out her name and then bursting into tears. Instead, I didn't have to do anything. She slowly reached out and wrapped her loving arms around me. She hugged me so tight it almost scared me. As she held me like that, it was hard to hold my emotions inside myself. Holding back the tears that were sitting on the edges of my eyelids was rather difficult, as I could picture myself bursting into tears and causing a scene that would surely be talked about throughout the whole town.

Her sweet voice, soft and light, muttered in my ear, "My sweet girl, you've finally come home. My heart has been longing for you." Then as she continued to squeeze me I heard the words *I've missed you so* flow from between her sweet beautiful lips.

She let me go and then took a step back. I couldn't take my eyes off her. She was so beautiful. More beautiful now than ever, I thought to myself. She stood taller than I remembered; her soft pale skin seemed to glow in the dim tavern light. Her long red curly hair was so beautiful. Long and flowing free down her back and around her body. I wanted to reach out and run my fingers through it. I wanted to reach out and hug her with all my might at that moment. I was so unsure of what to do. I felt sad but filled with love all at the same time. Her Irish green eyes had tears in them, which made me feel sad for leaving her in that small town, yet so glad that I was back to lay my eyes once again upon her beauty. I couldn't help myself any longer; I reached my hands out then wrapped my arms around her for one more hug. I breathed in the smell of her perfume as though it was going to be my last breath. With my cheek rested on her shoulder, my lips lightly whispered in her ear, "You look as wonderful as I remember." Then I asked, "Would you like to go somewhere to talk so we can catch up on the past three years?"

Her full, luscious red lips came close to my ear and I could feel the warm breath of her words upon my neck as she replied. "Yes, my darling, I would like that very much. I'll go anywhere with you. Oh how I've missed you so."

I suggested we go down to the Edgewater Motel, since that was where I had planned to rent a room anyway. She agreed that would be all right. I didn't know yet exactly what my plans were so I rented a room for a full week. I was undecided about signing up for more time in the military or going to a college somewhere. My indecisions led me to think that maybe I would just stay in that small town. My future was vague and unsettled. All I had really thought about during the past three years was Melissa and how I'd missed her. How I longed to be with her, to hold her, to love her. How maybe I'd made a mistake leaving her behind to go see at least part of the world. I'd needed to get away from everything that was wrong in my life because of living in that town. While I was in the military I realized all that was wrong in my life before had been so right. Loving that girl with long red hair and Irish green eyes was wrong in other people's eyes yet felt so right in my heart. I now understood so much more about myself. I understood why I loved Melissa so much. It wasn't only because of her beauty, her warmth, or her kind heart. It was because she made me complete. It was because of her love my heart kept beating the past three years.

As we entered the motel room my stomach felt like it could have been a small boat in a hurricane, twisting and churning. I was anxious to see what was about to happen with the love of my life and myself alone together for the first time in three years—not to mention in a motel room.

I placed my bag down in the chair next to the bed. She commented to me in a flirting way, "The military has been good to you. You look really sexy in that uniform."

I trembled inside as she took a small step toward me. Her hands reached up and started to peel my clothes off. We began breathing in unison as she pushed me down on the bed. Her soft, full lips then planted themselves firmly to my lips. Our mouths became one with each other. Neither of us wanted to let go to talk. It was as though we were both satisfied to be in one another's presence after being apart for so long. Our bodies wrapped together like a braided rope. We then proceeded to work one another's clothes off. Each of us could feel the moist heat rise from between our legs as our bodies became closer. That heat flowed with only the desire we held for each other. Our hands explored each other's bodies, soft and gentle, as if they were looking to find the center of each other's hearts. Our tongues still swimming fast and hard danced a dance of pure ecstasy. Her hands rubbed my inner thighs back and forth getting me even hotter. My hands teased through her long red hair and down the back of her neck, slowly finding their way around to the front of her body to her full breasts and hard nipples. With a soft touch of pure elegance I let my fingertips caress her nipples. Then I ran my knuckles up and down, back and forth, softly over them. The feel of her silky skin, smooth and warm to my gentle touch, was enough all on its own to give me an orgasm. Our bodies became sticky with sweat as they danced naked on that bed deep in passion. She then ran her tongue from one end of my body to the other. I felt it in and on more places than I ever had or even fantasized about before. Her fingers taunted my clit, touching me and stroking me until my legs opened wide and began to quiver. I could feel tension building up inside myself with the anticipation of her getting ready to love me. My stomach muscles tensed and my back arched at the same time when she inserted two fingers deep inside my wetness, pulling them in and out, in and out, over and over again. Then she pushed and pulled the two fingers in and out as her thumb encircled my swollen hard clit. I felt the release of my passions explode in her hand as I came like an exploding volcano. I took this opportunity to take her in a way I never had before. I slid my face down her body, tasting every inch of her with the tip of my tongue. With my arms locked around her body I rolled her over on the bed. I took a slow breath in to smell the sweet fragrance of that all-so-familiar perfume, which lingered in the air around her luscious body. At that moment her body began to call for me to love it with nurturing gestures. I then knew she was ready for me to love her, to love her with all my might. I had saved up a lot of passion in my heart from our years of absence from each other. I caressed her warm, soft, full breasts. I let my tongue circle one nipple then the other just before allowing it to travel down her body across her rippling taut stomach. The red curly hairs on her stomach just below her belly button tickled my nose slightly as my face continued its journey down her body. My lips stopped to kiss the hinge of her left hip. She let out a light moan of excitement. I then led my tongue down to explore her wetness. The taste of her hot wet womanhood held a flavor my taste buds had not tasted in so long. I then sank my tongue deep inside her; I heard her moan once again with excitement from being pleasured. I licked and flicked my tongue as soft and fast as I could across her wet hard clit to pleasure her like I knew she liked to be pleasured. The soft moans she cried from the pleasure I gave her satisfied my ears and only influenced me to love her all the more. I could feel her hands traveling up my back as I slid my body up hers. My mouth sucked on the nipple of her left breast before continuing up to her neck. Softly kissing her neck and holding her body tight felt so right. We held each other for a moment, pausing only to smile at one another in the excitement. Our eyes met for only a second or two just before the three little words of *I love you* escaped my lips and graciously rolled off my tongue as we continued to gaze into one another's eyes.

    We held and caressed each other for what seemed to be a long moment or maybe eternity. Our orgasms had cried in harmony as the hours passed while we loved one another that night. My lover was resting comfortably in my arms as the sun started peeking through the window upon us. I held her tight and admired her beauty for the longest time before I realized I was home, truly home. I was at the home where I wanted to stay. I wasn't going to run off to some college somewhere or take another tour of duty in the military. I would now choose a new duty, a tour of duty that meant keeping that sweet little redhead happy and satisfied for the rest of her life.

Just before I fell asleep, I smiled and my heart sang as she held me there. It was when she leaned in and whispered in my ear, "Welcome home, my sweet. . . . I love you, woman."

◆

THAT WAS TWENTY years ago yesterday. Today, I lay to rest my sweet red-haired Melissa. For after a year's battle with cancer, death has stolen her away from me. I know now at age forty-one my life is about to totally change. That my sweet girl with Irish green eyes and long red hair is now gone forever. As I look down to place a red rose on top of the cherrywood coffin, the tears begin to roll down my face. I start to realize a few more things. Along with the realization that the true tour of duty I vowed to do has now come to an unfortunate end, I realize that the last twenty-six years of my life will never be forgotten. That the loving memory I will carry of her will forever remain in my heart.

THE COLLISION OF COASTS

AIMEE HERMAN

THIS IS THE story of when a windshield meets paper. Not just any kind of paper. I'm not talking about a parking ticket or a handwritten note to alert you that your car has been hit while parked in a lot by someone who happened to overlook the size of their car against your car and a dent/scratch ensued. No, a different kind of paper. Allow me to set the scene.

Someone's garden is missing flowers because they were picked in such a way that the soil still drips from their stems and they smell of fertilizer, not flower shop. They are placed inside a newspaper page torn from its recycled casing. There is no interest to read the articles or advertisements printed on the page because there is already too much distraction. The flowers. Her handwriting. Purple marker, outlined and shaded in, of letters that equal a name that looked a lot like mine. Yes. *Me.*

Slowly, fingers unravel this delicate paper that has been reclaimed and reused so many times, I begin to make up stories of all the shapes it once was and colors and intentions. I wonder if I had ever touched this paper before as something else—a receipt maybe?

Beneath yellow flowers with drizzled petals was a photograph. Water against rocks. Blue merging into white foam. Imprinted ocean against sharp rocks. She writes about dreaming: *I hope you dreamed revolution.* My hands drip from enthusiastic imagination, picking up salt water paused by a camera lens, placed in my hand. She signs an initial as her name and I immediately decide that I have never seen such beautiful curves and lines represented by a symbol before.

It was not love at first letter, but it was something like that.

◆

THIS IS THE story of two coasts colliding, a deadline of days, the challenge of lost sleep. Our windshields became like mailboxes, as we placed tiny notes and longer letters into envelopes beneath windshield wipers. Invitations: Would you like to meet for coffee/tea/wine/beer? Declarations: Hello vowel, as hours pass I think about our feet walking over concrete squares. Malbec poured into ceramic mugs. Black sky lit up for our eyes to remember directions.

Sixteen days left of a school term. Final semester before summertime where plans pushed us in different locations and countries. East Coast and West Coast. The dilemma was this: we had two weeks together to learn and flirt and discover and lose sleep. We were competing with exams, papers, plans, and preparations. Some days, we met in the latest hours of night to walk her dog and talk about life and our own travelogue. Some days, we lived by notes—a constant stream of torn squares stuck to windows or pushed beneath doors. No matter what, the night always remained for us. She would creep inside my bedroom and slowly take off shoes, socks, clothes. My body woke immediately upon hearing her feet step against my carpet and lift herself into bed. When skin holds onto skin in such a way that nothing can get in the way. Not even a kiss—our lips were shy at times. We clung to shortened nights of sleep with closed eyes.

◆

WE MET ON a Saturday at a school event where creative expression was encouraged. As each scheduled person took the stage, I found my mind drifting. A woman in denim drag lip-synching to Bruce Springsteen. Two interpretive dancers who I could not seem to interpret. And then: *her*.

Tall bones enter the stage. Black cotton covering wide shoulders and the rest. A tie, loosely wrapped around her neck alternating in colors of blue and yellow. Jeans not allowing her shape to be seen. I envied her mystery. The microphone attempted to compete with her height, but she won. Her voice was deep and emotional. She spoke words of her history. Suddenly, the room was empty and my thoughts were removed, allowing room for only her fragments to fill me. I performed a piece about masturbation, which upon hindsight, I wish could have been something a bit more profound or enthralling.

The night ended as the lights grew brighter—a sign of the evening's culmination. I felt nervous and sweaty and searched for the right words to announce her impact on me. I could be wrong, but I'm quite sure it went like this:

(Redhead walks toward blonde, Dreadlocked Beauty sitting at a table conversing with friends. She takes a deep breath and forgets to let it out.)

Redhead: (. . .)

She thinks: QUICK! THOUGHTS! VOLUME! SOMETHING!

Redhead: Hhhhhhhhhhhhi.

Dreadlocked Beauty turns away from conversation and looks at Redhead, struggling with sentence structure.

D.B.: Hi.

R.: I . . . I um . . . I just wanted to tell you how much you . . . you . . . you really moved me when you were up there on stage. I was so . . . you were . . . um—

D.B.: Thank you. You were great up there too.

I do not know how to flirt, appear charming, accentuate my perfections. When in the presence of Dreadlocked Beauty, all I could do was stutter my words into an orgy of sounds not quite accumulating into much. I blew it.
Or so I thought.
I was walking out the door with my roommate and her friend and D.B. stopped me.
"Hey," she spoke.
What? Me? No, not me. Her. Someone. Anyone but me.
"Me?" I asked.
"Yeah. I just wanted to say how great it is to finally meet someone who speaks my language."
Meet someone? Me? Your language?
"Oh . . . uh . . . yeah . . . umm . . . thanksgreatmetoo."
On the car ride home, I couldn't stop talking about her. Something happened that night. Distracted my sleep and schedule. I didn't know her name or where she lived or even if she went to school there. Wouldn't I have seen her already? It was like she just appeared on stage out of nowhere.

◆

THIS IS A story of electronic inventions: computer screens and e-mail. Somehow she got my e-mail address and asked me for coffee sometime. Coffee turned into a pitcher of beer and a game of pool and a lot of talking. I learned her name and its origin. I told her about chopping all my hair off just a few months back because I wanted to *take back my curls* and the chaos that had stuck to them. I wanted to start over with new roots and length. I talked more than I ever had before with a stranger. Rather, I talked more about me and who I really am than I ever had before with a stranger. Although she never really felt like a *stranger* to me; there always remained an odd sense of home with her.

"I'm only here for sixteen more days," she said to me. "I work at a camp in the summer. It helps me pay for school."

I had learned that she was Canadian and unable to work in the U.S.

"Then we better savor these hours," I said.

◆

THIS IS A story of stamps and envelopes. Lots and lots of letters.

"Would you be interested in being my pen pal this summer?" she asked me one day while we were on one of our walks.

I could not contain my excitement. I was a huge fan of letter writing, though found myself never receiving any back. People were too busy for mailboxes and post offices. E-mails were much faster or text-messaging—allowing immediate response.

"Yes!"

◆

AND SO THE letters began. I went back east and worked in Brooklyn. I did not start a day without starting or completing a letter. She traveled with me to museums and parks. We took walks together, listened to music, shared deep secrets and troubles. All through my letters. I picked leaves and flowers from the ground and placed them inside envelopes alongside my words. I wrote on pictures and postcards, newspaper clippings, and receipts. I wanted her to experience each day with me.

When I would receive one of her letters, I'd hesitate opening it. First, I'd study the envelope: her drawings and handwriting, the postage, her ink. I would make sure that when I finally opened it up and read it, I was somewhere special (a park, my sister's stoop, a café where she could sit beside me—her words and I).

It was magic. Before the summer ended, I wrote and sent her forty letters. I had never given more words to anyone in my life.

◆

THIS IS A story of a road trip. She called me up one day after I had arrived back in town in early August.

"Would you like to drive back with me?"

She had driven to B.C. with a friend and wanted someone to take the trip back with her.

"Me? What about————or————or—"

"No one is able to. But besides that, I really would love to experience the drive with you. It's really beautiful."

"I don't know how to drive stick," I admitted.

"That's OK. I can teach you. And if you still can't, well then you can keep me company."

At first I said no. I couldn't afford the plane ticket to meet her half way. I didn't have a passport and wouldn't be able to meet her in Canada. The closest I would be able to come would be Spokane, Washington.

"I'll buy your ticket. Don't worry about the cost."

My mind continued to make up excuses because I was scared. We had spent all summer wrapped up in each other's words. Extreme intimacy. I worried it wouldn't be the same in person.

"Think about it. But, let me know soon, OK? If you can't, then I will need to find someone else."

I called my dad. He has seen me through several relationships—many of them more tumultuous than not. I knew he could help me make the right decision.

"Call her back right now and tell her yes," he said.

"But—"

"Don't make excuses. You've spoken about her all summer. It's magic. You need to follow that."

"But, I don't—"

"Call her."

◆

WE ALTERNATED DRIVING. I was nervous, but found highway driving easier, as it often remained within the same gear. I panicked in towns with traffic lights and stop signs. She was extremely patient and calm.

We made occasional bathroom stops and food breaks. One night, we camped at Yellowstone National Park, savoring burritos and Anne Sexton. We took turns reading poetry to each other when I found myself falling deeper and deeper in love. Before we fell asleep, our faces clung to one another. I thought we were going to kiss. I desperately wanted to kiss. And yet, we fell asleep wrapped in each other's warmth sans the locking of lips.

The sun steamed our windows open the next morning.

"Why didn't you kiss me last night," spoke my *good morning*.

"Why didn't *you* kiss *me?*"

The day was full of coffee and hot springs. Buffalo and beautiful landscapes. It was my first time at Yellowstone and I never could have imagined it to be more breathtaking.

◆

THIS IS A story of definitions and movement.

"So, are you my girlfriend?" I asked, while we arrived in a parking lot about to meet some friends for breakfast.

"I don't know—do you want to be?" she retorted.

And though this was not our first kiss, it felt larger, deeper, warmer, and longer.

"Yes!"

◆

SIX MONTHS (or thereabouts) later, we moved in together. All of a sudden, we were living in a space that had merged all of our things. Photographs, books, clothing, cookware. I didn't feel constricted. I enjoyed the unification of our lives through these *things*. She built a spice rack. I put things away. We were building a home. Creating a space of safety and love.

◆

THIS IS A story of beginnings and continuance. I graduated from college after almost a decade of ons and offs, of classes and commitments. We spent the summer together introducing our coasts.

"This is where I used to read your letters."

"I wrote to you while laying beneath this tree."

"Remember when I told you about that snap pea I picked and ate while talking with you on the phone? It was from this garden."

Introduction of stoops, addresses, family, friends, home.

✦

I FELL IN love with her stories. When she fingered out her dreadlocks, I fell in love with the new texture of her hair. Through sickness and health. Through extreme fights and disappointments. Fears and self-consciousness. Through the stresses of school, work, family, and life, I still remained.

And for that and many other reasons, I decided to take a different path one day on one of our walks.

First, she noticed the sign: IMAGINE: THE OCEAN.

Then, a nest of twigs and leaves with an egg sitting in the center. Or, more importantly, a ring dangling from one of the branches.

"Will you marry me?" I asked, no longer struggling for words like the very first day we met.

"Yes!"

S.O.A.R.

JOY PARKS

"YOU HAVE TO write about the kite," you said.

You said that everything true would not be believed. That everything that is fiction will seem real. And to never tell which is which.

It's still early but we've already had some rough moments. While I was making coffee this morning, I caught you looking at me fearfully, as if you weren't quite sure why I was there. You've been talking about flying east to get the rest of my things. You're worried that the plane will drop out of the sky, that horrible things will happen, that you will lose me forever. Still, we've come to the beach to fly a kite. It's one of the things we said we'd do. The thought of something left unfinished makes you even more anxious. You can't stand to deviate from a plan.

I sit beside you on the driftwood and watch you struggle to put the kite together. You're terrible at anything like this. I think of that Sunday you spent attaching a light fixture to the kitchen wall. How the air was blue with curses and the backsplash pocked with tiny, uneven holes. You thought it was hilarious and offered me a chance to trade up for some butch with better handi-dyke skills.

That was when you still felt safe enough to make offers like that.

This morning I remembered how years ago, long before we were lovers, you once told me that someday I wouldn't need you anymore. You said a time would come when I would want to be free to fly on my own. That was the first time you ever made me cry.

I'm laughing at you because the kite won't come together. You're laughing too, and you touch my knee and tell me you're OK right now. Not crazy. At least not for these few moments. You suggest that I keep a record, like the tide tables one finds in every restaurant and store here. Break the day into five-minute increments, chart out the parts of the day when you're not crazy. I'm glad we can talk about it like this, make jokes. Say the word. *Crazy.* But that's the problem, isn't it? It's too easy for you to let me in; you have no protection against me. You can sleep with me in your bed through the night. Hang our clothes in the same closet. We tell each other things neither of us has ever told anyone. This is the kind of intimacy you always wanted. Now it's the thing that scares you the most.

You say you fear losing yourself in me. I think you fear whom you might find.

I don't know it now, but one night soon, you'll fall asleep after loving me, your fingers still inside my body. And I will lie as still as I can, not wanting to wake you. Not wanting this to end. I don't know it now, but I will think about this night months from now, shiver at the memory of your hands. Be glad that my body could give you the kind of peace and rest you longed for, the sense of being wanted that you were denied for so long.

I slide over a little closer to you, listen to you mumble at the kite. Feel your warmth at my arm, like a guard against the dampness and the cool air. I wish you could understand that this is enough. That I could sit here beside you forever and not need anything more. That I can love you enough to deal with whatever happens. But there is no way for me to make you believe this.

Finally you finish. We celebrate that you have managed to put the kite together with no instructions; we comment on how pretty the colors are. You're thrilled that there are only a few small stray pieces left over, their purposes still a mystery. Then you hand me the kite. Like an order. I look at you in mock helplessness and ask what you expect me to do with it.

"Fly it," you say. "I did my part. Now let's see if you can get it into the air."

I don't know it now, but I will spend hours thinking about another day on another beach. I will think about how, after chasing each other throughout the country for years, decades really, missing each other only by days at times, you took me to the greenest field I've ever seen, on a cliff hanging above a rocky and wild stretch of ocean. And we stood here at this edge of the world and you shouted above the wind that you loved me and slipped a ring on my finger, the only engagement ring you've ever bought. And you kissed me and somehow you thought all the pain and the past would disappear. That the years between us would fall away and we'd be just two kids from Queens who happened to fall in love. You told me you felt worthy, finally, of being loved and you hummed "Somewhere" from West Side Story *and called me your New York femme. You believed you had loved me in a past life; believed too, that you had finally found me, claimed me once again just before it was too late.*

You liked the idea of us being fated. It made decisions unnecessary.

When I stand up, a gush of wind flares and pushes the kite into my chest. I stagger backwards a few steps. It's heavier than I expected, clumsier. I have no idea what to do or how to launch it. I look over at you; you've strolled a few feet away. You're poking the sand with your walking stick, as if I'm no longer there.

I watch you step carefully in the sand. Your limp is more pronounced when you're sad or scared. And you're both today. Still, you're doing better than before, something you remind me of often. Now you only need your stick for sand or rocks. I'm very careful about not calling it a cane. But today you are stiff, holding yourself close and rigid, walking slowly. The wind is coming faster now and stronger; soon the tide will begin pushing the ocean toward us. Maybe some rain. I don't want you to get cold. Time to fly.

I double-check the huge spool of string attached to the kite and grab the wooden frame where it forms a cross. There's more than enough wind. If I throw it into the air and can get some lift, all I have to do is roll out the line, let the kite float on the gusts that keep pushing me backwards. I stop and look at you again. I'm not sure why I'm hesitating. It's just a kite. You look over, expectant, squinting against the gray light soaking through the clouds. You look like you're waiting for something important to happen.

When we were first learning to love each other, you spoke of us as a kite and a tether. You made up a holiday that only we could celebrate and bought me a painting of kites flying in the wind. You warned me that you preferred to hold tight to the ground; said you could only offer me a place to land. Something solid to fly home to. You were so afraid of anchoring me, my life just taking off, loving me enough to want me to be free to fly. You told me to soar. But eventually your warnings stopped. And one night when you were brave and not my anchor, but my lover, I whispered, "Let's both be kites," and you agreed. *This is how we talked to each other. This is how we fell in love. Maybe I went too far in wanting you to be a kite with me.*

You want to fly so badly, but you're too afraid of falling to manage to get off the ground.

I throw the kite into the air, and immediately the wind catches the underside. I watch in awe as it rises, then remember the reel of string under my arm. I take it in both hands, one hand on each handle. The kite spins upward, pulls hard. I wasn't prepared for it to take off so easily. I love the way it pulls, jerks me upward, stretches me. I didn't expect it to feel like this. As I spin the reel, I can feel the tug grow more urgent. I wonder how much string is on the reel. Probably plenty, it's your string, your kite; you're usually prepared for anything. You say it's all these years of living in the country. I think it's just the natural-born Girl Scout in you. The kite keeps climbing and I keep unrolling more string, occasionally calling out for you to look. I want you to see what I've accomplished.

And you do, your head tossed back, your cap nearly falling off, your one hand up to shield your eyes against the strange gray daylight, the other behind you, gripping the walking stick. You smile, first at the kite, then back at me; it's a real smile, one that comes from inside you when the darkness lifts and clears for a while, maybe from some distant place where the darkness hasn't penetrated. Not yet anyway.

It dawns on me at this point, all I have to do is to hold the string and ride out the wind. So I loosen my grip, settle into the task, relax a little. The kite is still climbing, bouncing through the sky, trembling and pulling as if it's trying to break free. I try to calculate how high it is, figure at least a couple of hundred feet. Maybe as high as a city high-rise, that's how I still measure things. I glance over at the looping spans of bridge that cross the water; it's nearly as high as that, maybe higher, hard to tell. Higher than I ever imagined I could fly it. I loosen my grip even more. A rush of wind lifts the kite straight up; I'm holding the reel with both arms up in the air, stretching hard. You yell something to me, but I can't make it out. All I hear is how you say my name. That's all that carried on the rush of wind.

Beloved. Lover. Womanlove. Smart-ass. My grand passion. My brainy chick. My girl.

These are the things you called me. This is what I was to you. I think of how you reached for me across a country.

In the dark, you whisper how much you love me. Stroke my hair. Beg me not to break your heart. I've never known a woman more born to be a suitor. You say my name over and over like a litany; there's something holy about this, sacred. Your need of me so strong, you never expected it to be like this, never expected how real and deep it would be, so much more than what you believed was possible. I think about how defenseless I am to you and how open, how easy for me to tell you what I want. That I want you. I hear my name turning over in your mouth, like a taste, my legs opening. I'm giving you my body. You're taking my heart.

You wander away from the patch of beach grass and weeds, stroll down closer to the water where the sand is still wet. Your steps are light; you leave no path. The clouds break and watery sunlight hits the waves. The kite is flying. You're not crazy right now. It's hard not to feel happy. I want to hang on to this moment, chew all the flavor out of it, save the memory of it. This, the kite in the air, the sun and the ocean, and you smiling. It's enough. I watch you start to sketch out some letters with your walking stick; you're writing something in the sand. I stand up on my toes to see, afraid to move forward too much, afraid that I will change something, disturb this balance. Bring the kite crashing down. You draw a wide arching circle with your stick, enclosing the letters. Then you turn to me, watch me strain to read what you have written. And you smile again. That smile. It's addictive. The things I've done to see that smile.

I don't know it now, but I'll never be able to eat cotton candy again. Or pecans or really good bread or date bars or salt water taffy. I don't know that there will be songs I can't listen to, movies I can't watch, even clothing I won't be able to wear again. Our mythology touched everything; it's too huge to bear at times. But it's the cotton candy that stays with me and I'll remember your lusty comments on what could be done with it, the country fairs you promised me, how you wanted to elope with me in Vermont, buy quilts, drive across the country after years of barely leaving your house. Make love in seedy, cheap hotels in every state. Everything becoming sensual, sexual, a way to connect. The heat of your imagination when it was turned up high, the string that ran between your intellect and your lust. How I instinctively knew how to follow that path, heat you with words. I will think of cotton candy, fragile spinning strings of colored sugar, how it flies out from the edges and you can't catch it, can't hold it; I will think of how it melts away, taste left like a memory on your tongue. And I will think about you.

We watch the kite for a long time. I'm out of string but it doesn't matter, it's so high, and the wind current seems to be keeping it up there without any help from me, waves of ocean air making it skip and dart and toss. I'm not thinking about anything else but right now. This moment, this day, this kite. You smiling. It's something I've learned to do lately, a way to trick myself into not worrying about what comes next. But there's a patch of dark purple cloud moving toward us, rain following the low tide. It doesn't matter. We did it. We flew a kite together just as we said we would. Time to bring it in, take it down, and go home. Get on with the day.

What I don't know now is that you will try to keep things as normal as possible. That you'll send me presents, kitchen stuff for the home of my own I don't have the heart to set up, the bubblegum charms I love, tiger's-eye on a gold chain to protect me, notes authored by the cats and cards with funny rabbits and e-mail almost every day. But you'll never ask me if I hurt or if I'm lonely. You can't. And you never tell me that you don't love me. I don't know now that this will make everything so much harder.

I start spinning the reel carefully, trying to keep it even. Getting the kite down isn't going to be that easy. I strain a little against the upward pull, slowly drawing in the string, hundreds of feet of it, inch by inch. The kite is jerking wildly, buffeted by breezes I can't feel down here. Now that the kite has had a taste of flight, it's going to fight to stay in the air. You're behind me now and to my right; I turn for just a moment to watch you watching first me, then the kite, then me again. You're feeling the struggle, anticipating the landing, the ending to this. You're still smiling; you're still OK.

You told me I was your memory. Charged me with the task of recalling details for you. So I worry that what was good about us will get pressed flat in your mind, rolled over. Erased. I don't want you to forget the way we laughed at dinner, sitting close, hands resting on the cool Formica. How we slow-danced to an old Johnny Rivers tune in front of the kitchen sink. I'm scared that you won't remember how it felt to touch me, the way we cried out to each other, the words we spoke when we made love. I worry that with each morning that you wake in the room you once couldn't sleep in without me, with each sunset you don't report to me in a hundred different kinds of pink and blue and peach, I will fade.

You really haven't forgotten that much. The only things that get lost are the things that don't matter. I am afraid of becoming one of those things.

It would appear that I have everything under control. Until the kite is hovering no more than twenty feet above me. Then it happens. A huge gust of wind, some strange ocean current, something blustery and unexpected, jerks the reel from my hand. I'm too surprised to react as quickly as I should. My fingers open. I let go, barely believing I could do this so easily, be so careless. This has been so perfect, I feel like I've ruined it somehow. The kite string dangles in front of me, just slightly out of reach, so I start moving forward, slowly at first, as if chasing the kite will make it move faster, run further from me. It teases me. It feels as if I could simply reach out and grab the string and pull it in, back to me. But I know it's just an illusion.

You've moved farther ahead up the beach and you're yelling something at me, but the wind is blowing too hard; I can't hear you. Your hands are in your pockets; you're watching to see what I'll do. It's really moving now; the kite is starting to arc higher in the sky, the string bouncing ahead of me; soon it will be completely out of reach. So I run, but the sand is dry and I keep sinking; I can't move that fast. As I run past you I can feel you watching me, your one hand still up, shading your eyes. You're probably getting upset. I'm getting tired and I start to slow down, my eyes still fixed on the string that keeps drifting away. Finally, I stop and bend over to get my breath. The kite is flying away and I don't know how to get it back.

I don't know it now, but there will be nights when the pain is so bad, so close, when it presses down so hard I can't breathe. I don't know yet that the worst times will come at twilight, just as the light fades away, the time of day you too were lonely, and I'll remember the Bob Dylan song we would mouth to each other about evening shadows and the stars and fears. And holding each other for a million years. It doesn't seem possible right now, but eventually I will find myself getting from one day to the next, that whole hours will go by without thinking about you. I don't know now how angry and scared I will get or how sometimes I will hope for the day when you don't come and rest on my mind. Or that losing you this way will hurt most of all.

That's why it takes me a minute or two to realize what's happening. Bits of dry sand splash my coat; I hear your footsteps smacking the ground. I look up and you're running. You're running. You could barely walk last year, and now you're running past me up the beach. There's a pained look on your face, but you're running and you're yelling at me as you run past and I still can't make out a thing you say, but I don't care, it doesn't matter. You're running. That's all that counts.

You chase the dangling kite string up into the beach grass. It's right in front of you and I actually believe at that moment that you will catch it. Then you look at me and you smile, it's a tremendous smile, a brave smile, the kind of smile I waited years for you to smile at me. Then in one sudden gust, the wind lifts the kite higher than you can reach. It's slipped away after all that, gone for good now. You shrug your shoulders and grin and turn and watch it fly. It's beautiful, the rainbow of color rising higher and higher, drifting and tilting upward over the ocean. It looks so free. You are saying something; I see your mouth move. But I'm not sure you're talking to me.

I don't know it now but I won't be able to forget your voice. How you used to say, "I love you, I love you, I love you." Always three times, like an omen, as if your words could keep me safe. I don't know how badly I will want to believe you did this for the right reasons, that this was the most selfless thing you've ever done. Your last act of protecting me.

I walk up the beach to meet you. You don't say anything, you simply slip your arm around me, shove your hand into the back pocket of my jeans, press your cheek against mine. I think I feel a tear but I honestly can't tell if it's yours or mine. We watch the kite pause, light on some treetops on the tiny bit of ground and rocks across the inlet from us. I turn and watch you watching the kite, the wonder in your eyes, and the sadness too, so deep inside that I can't reach it. I love you and there's nothing I wouldn't do for you. Now I know what that means. I know what I have to do.

When I turn back to the sky, the kite is gone.

Finally, we turn and start walking down the beach; you're grinning and shaking your head. I quietly tell you I'm sorry that I lost the kite. You laugh at me and kiss my hair and tell me it doesn't matter. Not at all. You say it doesn't matter because today I soared and you ran and that's worth losing a kite. That's worth everything. I know you really believe that.

I don't know it yet, but the day I fly away, you'll find it hard to leave the airport. You'll cry for nearly thirty miles straight on the drive back and come home to a new kite perched on the bed. Our bed. Now yours. You'll write and tell me you think it's beautiful, tell me that I'm so thoughtful; you'll tell me that you want to hang it on the wall in the spare room. You want me to know that you understand how important this is.

Your face changes, grows serious. Your voice is raspy from running, but warm, so warm and you tell me that you pick this as the closing scene in the movie about us. I turn to look at you, your hair blown back in the wind, your eyes the brightest blue I've ever seen them, your cheeks flushed from either running or being excited about being able to do it. I take your hand; it feels cold. I raise it to my mouth, brush your fingers with my lips. I wish that I were older. That I could have met you when you were younger. That I had known you before all those things that happened to you, the things that make us impossible. You squeeze my hand. "We'll have them sobbing in the aisles," you whisper.

I don't know it now, but this is the day I lost you. There on the beach, when we both found the last thing we needed from each other. The day you ran. And I soared.

On the way to the car, you tell me to put my hand in your pocket. While I was flying the kite, you were gathering agates and beach glass; you have some sort of particular magic when it comes to finding treasures that splash their way up onto the sand. So I move closer to you, slide my hand inside your jacket pocket. I feel the outline of hip beneath your coat, the taut muscles of your runner's thigh still solid and firm. I know this game. I can have whatever precious rock I pick out but I have to go by touch only. I stop, graze your leg again with my hand, smile; you grin back, draw in your breath, shudder with pleasure that I'm this close, touching you. I still have that kind of power over you. You kiss me, my hand still deep in your pocket. You slide your arms around me inside my coat. I'm close enough to feel your heart beat, feel your breathing. You press your wind-chapped cheek against mine. There is nothing in the world that feels this good. We hold each other like that for a while, until I remember the stone I've gripped in my hand inside your pocket. You let go of me slowly and when I open my hand and look down, it's a large stone, a blue agate, almost the color of your eyes in that light. A chunk of ocean, both fragile and solid, and sharp on the edges.

I don't know it now, but I will hang on to that stone like an amulet, I will hold it in my hand all through the flight back east. Once I get settled, I will take it to a jewelry store and have a fitting attached to it, wear it around my neck every day. Sometimes, when I turn quickly, when I forget that it's there, it will scrape against my skin. Startle me with a sharp, unexpected pain. It will start to leave a mark just below my throat. But that won't be enough to make me take it off.

On the way home, we drive over the bridge that spans the beach. I look down and see what you wrote while I was flying the kite: S.O.A.R. And I realize that it's a heart you've drawn around the letters, not a circle. A heart. With the most loving word you know spelled out inside it. I reach over, touch your shoulder. You pat my hand, smile, stare straight ahead at the road. Blink back tears. You know I understand the importance of this. That no matter what happens from this point on, I know you have loved me as best you could, better than you ever thought possible. I know that even though you had little left to give, you gave it, you risked everything for me and loved me deeper and sweeter and more completely than most women could dream of being loved. And that's enough. It has to be.

"Soar," you would tell me when some bureaucratic roadblock stood between us. "Soar," you would say when my ex drained my bank account. "Soar," you whispered when my mother's shrill selfishness wounded me. "Soar above it all my love. Be who you were meant to be. Don't let anyone bring you down. Soar and fly home to me."

We drive across the bridge and you tell me that I need to write about this day, that nothing will make sense until one or both of us does. I don't want you to know that I'm crying now so I turn my head and take a final look back at your s.o.a.r. You have given me instructions. What I have to do. I imagine movie credits running over the back of the car as we drive away into the distance. I almost expect to see the tip of the kite rise like a nod, over the hills, some sort of good-bye. But that would be too perfect. And I realize that this is as close as we are supposed to get to perfection.

So I soar.

Because otherwise, all of this happened in vain. We happened for a reason. So I could soar. And so you could run, briefly, on a beach on a windy day in the spring on legs that would barely hold you six months before. But that's reason enough. So I soar. Sometimes without direction, sometimes with broken wings, sometimes low and shaky and unsure because the pain drags me down. I soar because you found the courage to chase love and kites, even if only for a short distance. Because you trusted a heart and legs that had failed you so many times before. So I have to do the same. Be worthy of what you gave me. I soar because loving you taught me that the best kind of love is the kind that takes you and throws you and your world into the air, shakes you up, without a single thought about where you'll land. And that doesn't matter; you have to give in, let it raise you up, let it make you brave. Let it take you where you are meant to go.

So I soar. Because that is the only way I have left to love you.

MISFIRE

LORI HICKS

FIRST I FEEL her lips, their wet softness travels from my hips along my stomach, up my torso to the ticklish part of my neck. Fifteen years and she can still cause my skin to dance with excitement as her mouth searches for mine. Our lips press together harder than usual, more compressed, not soft or supple, forced it seems, and rather brief. Then she lays her warm body on mine—only momentarily—before rolling on her side and then slowly moving onto her back. That's when I feel it . . . Ashley's hand. Until now, it was like Landon and I were the only two in our bed. For a fleeting moment it almost feels like old times again, just the two of us making love. Something I am beginning to miss.

Ashley's hand continues to do a token massage of my breasts as she moves on top of Landon, who is now sandwiched between Ashley and me. I slightly adjust myself to get more involved with the fervor that brushes up next to me. I begin stroking Ashley's backside and I allow my tongue to tickle the nape of Landon's neck. I feel the heat rising from her skin, hoping it is I who arouses her; I look up. That's when I notice she is swiveling her hips and pressing her body tight against the youthful body of Ashley. I see Landon's mouth wildly searching for Ashley's as her passion consumes this newcomer. No one even notices as my touch diminishes, but my stare does not. I watch the new recruit make love to my partner. It seems her hands are suddenly everywhere at once. She strokes and probes my wife as I willingly watch. I observe the sparks fly as the electricity makes Landon's body arch with energy. I watch Ashley's inquisitive fingers rouse Landon's body around my bed as I move away from them. It seems Ashley is causing Landon to explode with a passion I have not yet seen, an energetic burst of sexual energy that has not ever surfaced in our fifteen years.

I hear a yearning moan coming from Landon; like a bullet to the head, it ricochets in my brain. Her soft whine that has so often stirred me toward climax now sickens me as I watch her throat arch and her head dig into the pillow with pleasure.

I decide to move away from them, far away. "Hey," I say without looking at them. "I'm goin' to the bathroom. . . . You two feel free to finish this. Whatever *this* is?" I mumble while quickly walking out of the room.

My legs tremble; barely able to carry myself across the floor, I stumble through the threshold of my consciousness as I move into the restroom. I am feeling physically ill, almost as if I'll faint. The perspiration builds on my face. I shut the door and fall to my knees in front of the toilet. My mind spins around the bathroom, my mental picture stuck on Landon and Ashley making love. It's like a horror film in slow motion, with a ridiculous X-rated, bass-thumping melody that pounds in my head. We have done it a few other times before now, the three of us. I've always felt included before this, never comfortable but in no way rejected. Up to now, I'd say I was even a bit intrigued.

We met Ashley on the Internet a few months back. Nice girl, but she's young, even younger than Landon. She was pretty in the picture. Her short blonde hair framed her face nicely. She wasn't really a dyke, but nor was she femme either. Landon and I actually laughed at that. Landon is more butch, not that she is unfeminine. Let's just say she does the yard work and I clean the house. We thought it was funny how Ashley was desirable to both of us in some way. Her dating profile alleged she liked many of the same things we did, like hiking, and bike riding, in fact nature in general. Traveling was something she didn't do much, but wanted to. She loved animals and old people, and had no children, same as us. In big bold letters on Ashley's site, it said she was open-minded, not looking for a serious relationship, and it also mentioned she was adventurous to a fault. Besides her soft features and kind smile, these were things that attracted us to Ashley. Let's face it, not everyone advertises *three-ways are welcome*. That is the only reason Landon and I were on the dating site to begin with. So, zesty keywords like *adventurous* and *open-minded* peppered our opinion of her. I'm beginning to think a three-way was not such a good idea.

I grab some Kleenex off the back of the toilet. Then I clear my throat and I spit in the water. I wipe my mouth and my tearing eyes before flushing, and then I rise. Shuffling over to the sink, I wash my hands while intently looking into the mirror. All I see are the dark, sunken, green eyes of a stupid fool looking back at me. My natural curly hair is mussed from my fingers frantically running through it, giving me the look of a mad woman. I have never felt so idiotic. It is so bad I must turn away from my own reflection. I cannot bear to look at my dim-witted self anymore. Suddenly I am dizzy. I try to keep the room from spinning, so I close the lid of the toilet to park myself. It seems I sit forever, naked and dumbfounded. I am taken aback by the emotion I witnessed erupting from my lover. A sensation I was afraid she was no longer able to experience since the loss of her parents. Poor things, they died healthy, dreadfully, unexpectedly in a house fire, both of them gone, just like that, no good-byes.

Why hasn't Landon walked into the bathroom yet? She should be coming to look for me by now. Christ, how long does it take to have an orgasm? My head pounds with the answers to my own questions. *Why, why, why?* My mind twists my thoughts. I glance down and notice my reddened hands clenching. With whitened knuckles, my nails dig deep into the tops of my thighs, causing blood to trickle from a slight opening in my pale skin. One pain momentarily helps me feel relief from another. I rise and look around the small room for something besides a towel to wrap my pastel white body. Finding nothing, and opting not to go out with a shower curtain as a cover up, I jerk a towel off the rack and drape myself. Still fuming, I head back through the door. I'm sure I'm going to find them in the final throes of passion, maybe not even aware I ever left the room. I immediately put my head down; never looking up, I cross the room toward our closet. I stand staring into the open doorway.

First, I feel her breath, hot and moist. My gaze remains forward on the clothes rack, briefly, before journeying up. There it is on the shelf; I see the gun, our loaded protector. I never wanted it, the gun that is, but Landon did. Something else I uncomfortably gave in to. The revolver has always been there, but for some reason I notice it more now than I have the thousands of other times before. I feel Landon's open mouth kissing my neck. Her hands wrap my waist. Her head rests on my back.

"Babe, what's the matter?" Her tone comes across as caring, but her touch seems to be forced. With her breathy words the stench of old beer travels to my senses.

I tense my body; quickly becoming rigid, I don't turn around. "Why would you ask that?" I say. I feel her hand tugging on my arm. My blurred focus lingers on the polished pearl handle tucked under a cowboy hat on the shelf. I picture the weapon in my hands, gun to my head. Finally, overcoming the urge, I look away from the handgun. I struggle to reach for a shirt as she tries turning my body to face her. I'm feeling extremely upset. How could Landon enjoy it that much? How could she humiliate me like that?

"Why did you get up and leave Ashley and me?" she asks in a broken whisper. "Turn around, Nic. Look at me."

I pull my shirt over my head. "I just wasn't into it tonight, that's all. I wasn't feelin' it, Landon."

I remember the first time Landon called me Nic, my heart melted. She had a smooth way about her that attracted attention, especially mine. Her voice, her tone; she cast a spell with her sound that echoed sweetness when she spoke. Everyone called me Nicole or Nicky, but Nic was a pet name only Landon used. One she often used to express excitement, or when she wanted something. And right now she apparently wants something. I finally turn around. Landon stands before me, her naturally tan body naked under a half-buttoned flannel shirt.

"Where's our new sex toy?" I ask, trying to curve my lips into a fake smile. The fire in my eyes burns past her. I look around the room furiously. "I hope she didn't leave on my account?" I push past Landon as I move toward my pants on the chair next to the bed. I can't bring myself to look into her eyes, so I face the wall, staring into them anyway. A large frame hangs with a picture of Landon and me on the top of Devil's Rock. Our eyes are bright with achievement, our smiles wide with exhilaration. Happier times, much happier; our smiles are proof of that.

"Why are you freaking out?" she asks, ignoring both of my questions. "You said you were OK with all this. You agreed we needed to spice up our love life. It was your idea. All I did was go along with it. Why are you suddenly acting so hurt by it all? You're acting jealous."

"Jealous . . ." I repeat, while slipping into my jeans. I gasp at the word, or is it the struggle to button my pants that takes my breath away. "Why? Should I be jealous?" I push back. It seems there is a discharge of electricity in my head, *Jealous—Jealous—Jealous.* The words flash in my mind like lightning in a thunderstorm. Until now she has always made me think being ten years older was no problem. "I mean, you always said you liked older women, right? If so there is nothing for me to be jealous of." I use my most confident tone even as my skin radiates green. I suddenly feel ancient. My throat throbs with the letters *O-L-D.*

"Look at me!" Landon shrieks, while forcefully spinning my body around.

I attempt to avoid her stare, but I fail. Filled with intention, her dark eyes search me out. She grips me tight and tells me straight out, "It's not what you think it is." Suddenly it is *her* eyes darting around the room as she pulls me into her chest.

How does she know what I think it is? I shove back a little, uncomfortable with her grip. I look at her perfect complexion, her ink black eyes, and the narrow shape of her lips as she searches for words. Landon's short dark hair falls forward, outlining her fine features.

"This was all in fun, Nic. If you're not having fun anymore we can stop. I did this for you," she says in a silky voice, pulling me back to her. "Don't do this. Don't look at me like that." The sweetness in her voice is thick as she wraps her arms around me and hugs me tight.

I seem to calm, relaxing my head slightly on her shoulder. I speak softly, "OK, maybe I overreacted a little. I admit I just—" I stop midsentence, looking over near the doorway. I am stunned by my vision.

"Is everything all right? I thought I heard your voices getting loud." Ashley walks into the bedroom carrying three beers. "I thought a drink might be nice for everyone."

All of a sudden, it feels like my head is in a vice. Rapidly, my relaxed state is replaced with an excruciating degree of fury. My eyes glare past Landon as I push her back and pin my sight on Ashley. Her bright eyes shine; her smile is wide, obviously unaware of the anger that flares between lovers.

"What's wrong, Landon? Did you tell her?" Ashley asks with an expectant tone. She stands in a robe that loosely drapes her thin, naked body. The robe was a present I gave Landon for Christmas last year.

I notice Landon's head snap back to Ashley, her eyes narrowed, capturing Ashley's glare. I find their fleeting look to be a signal of some sort.

"What?" I scream out. "What is it you were supposed to tell me, Ashley?" I try hard to pry her eyes off Landon without sounding too desperate. "I am surprised to see you. I thought you knew enough to leave."

Landon tries again with a desperate tone. "Babe, you are overreacting. Ashley's—"

Suddenly, Ashley interrupts Landon. "Is there something I'm missing here?" Ashley sets the three bottles on the dresser and begins searching for her clothes.

I'm the one who should be upset, yet Ashley is the one who now has attitude and is flying around the room.

"That's it," says Ashley. "I'm out of here," she says, flailing her arms. "This kind of thing always happens. Someone always gets hurt. I don't need it."

"How would you know?" I stare in her direction, my eyebrows arched high on my face. "Is this a common occurrence for you? Do you make it a habit of tearing apart lives, Ashley? You made us believe this was the first time." I can no longer fake a smile, or my tone. I am outraged by her slighted manner, and my pitch and expression articulate that.

Ashley puts on her blouse and steps up to my face, so close I swear I can smell Landon on her skin. "Hey, Nicole," she says. "Remember who called who? Don't blame me for your screwed up life. If you hadn't already messed it up you'd never have needed me." Turning away from my enraged stare she steps into her pants and looks back at Landon. "You are married to a nut job, Landon. Who is this person? Where did 'Nicole' go?" She sarcastically looks around the room.

"Stop, both of you." Landon walks toward me and whispers, "She's right, babe, you are not yourself. Have you been taking your medication?"

Immediately, I push back. I feel the tension in my features. I struggle for breath, hearing her words slap me over and over. *She's right. She's right. She's right.* I thrust forward into Landon, pushing her back; I yell loudly, "Why do you have to ask about that?" I watch as Landon falls backward over Ashley and onto the floor of our bedroom. In my rage I don't notice Ashley bending down behind Landon, putting on her shoes. "You know I've been fine." I look down at her. "Why do you want to bring that up? Why now? Why now? Why now?" I hear myself repeating the words aloud. "Every time we have issues you want to bring up the medication. Like it's some sort of miracle drug or something. Is that what you and your little girlfriend talk about?" My skin is heating up. I can feel warmth rising from my scalp. The thought runs through my head, *I have been doing so well I decided not to take the medication anymore.* But, I don't dare tell her. I say to myself quietly as I look at Landon: *I don't need the meds anymore.* I want to surprise her. I want to show her.

Landon picks herself up from the floor and comes back at me. "You need to sit down. You are not acting right. When I look in your eyes, it's as if you're not there." Landon is in my face.

"I'm leaving." Ashley's screeching voice shatters my train of thought. She stands abruptly and moves toward the bedroom door.

Suddenly the room closes in, my chest crushes my lungs for breath, and all I hear are my own words, "Oh, no you're not!" My words reverberate as I leap toward the closet and grab the gun. I quickly turn and point it at the two women who have just made love in my bed. I can see the shocked look on their faces as they stare down the barrel. Caught. They are guilty and I have found them out. The figures before me go out of focus. My body wobbles and my ears burn.

"Nic, what are you doing?" Landon's voice doesn't sound true.

"Don't call me that. Only Landon calls me that."

"Honey, I am Landon. . . . Put the gun down please."

"I want out of here." I hear a voice cry out from the back of the room.

I point the gun to my head. "Why, Landon? Why did you stop loving me? Am I not good enough for you? I was there for you. I was there for you when they died. I carried you when your parents died. I've always been there for you, Landon. How could you do this to me after fifteen years?"

"Landon, you told me it was Nicole's parents who died?" Ashley's shrill voice rings loud in my head.

"Ashley, you should go. Just walk out the door, Ashley. Now!" Landon's voice is piercing. Almost knifelike I feel her stabbing me with the name *Ashley*.

"No!" I scream loud and point the gun back in their direction. "I want to know what the two of you were planning." A shadow moves toward me; my vision is impaired by my fury.

Bang! An earsplitting shot rings loud; screams echo in my head. . . .

"You shot her! All she wanted to do was help you and you shot her!" I hear a frantic voice screaming in the background of my faded vision. "I'm calling 911. Jesus, Nicole. She loved you." The sobbing noise moves toward the bedside table. "Why did you shoot Landon? You may have killed her. We must move quickly to try and save her."

Killed her? Killed her? Killed her? The words finally register. "Oh my God!" I scream at the top of my lungs. "How could I shoot Landon! How did the gun go off?" I glance down, tears streaking my face. I howl my pain. "What just happened? Did I kill her? Is she dead?" I stare into the childlike eyes of Ashley. "Is she dead?" I repeat loudly. It is as if I briefly left the room and returned to this horrific scene. I look and I can finally see clearly. Landon lies unconscious on the floor.

Blood pulsing from her midsection, her moan is now a painful grumble. I stand with the .38 revolver clenched between the fingers of my dangling arm.

"I am not leaving her. Kill me if you must," says Ashley, kneeling beside Landon, "but I'm staying. The ambulance is on its way."

"Why didn't she come for me? Why didn't Landon come get me from the bathroom? What were you guys doing all that time?"

"All what time? What do you mean?" Ashley looks at me with puzzled judgment. "You were only gone like two minutes. I got up and was going to get a drink when you came out of the bathroom. Landon had just told me she loved you too much to continue. I was going to have a farewell beer and leave, that's all. You know she only did it for you. It was all for you, Nicole." She screams her words. "Landon knew you wanted a change after losing your parents. She knew it devastated you the way they both died at the same time, so tragically and all."

My parents . . . dead? I ask myself. Then as I stare blankly into the face of Ashley, the flood of memories rushes in, the pictures of my childhood, our family holidays together, the fire, the burned bodies and charred remains of my family home. And their funeral, the friends, the family, me and Landon, and yes, it is my parents who are gone; I see that now.

Ashley turns away from my gaze. "Please, Landon . . . Please hold on." I see her desperate eyes as she pleads with the bloodied body. Then she looks up at me and begins to speak again. This time her tone is regretful. "Landon had asked me to leave. She told me this was it. There would be no more of the three of us. She and I stopped the minute you left the room, Nicole. I'm the one who insisted on one more beer. I'm the one who thought everything was all right." Ashley is mumbling through her sobs. "Why didn't I just leave?" Her words are a faint whisper as she questions herself, her gaze now on Landon.

I look down at the young woman we met on the Internet; I watch as she cries in hysterics over Landon's bleeding body, and in a meek voice I ask her, "You were leaving, huh? She told you she still loved me?" I can hardly look at Landon. I pray it's not too late. All I want to do is beg for her forgiveness. I can't believe my enormous misfire. I hear myself repeatedly screaming the words, "I'm sorry, I'm sorry, I'm sorry!" Lastly, I do look at Landon, and I quietly whisper, "I love you . . ." I raise the gun to my head and I pull the trigger.

"Doctor, Doctor, look, Nic just opened her eyes." I look up and I see Landon, my charming, beautiful Landon; her eyes roam over my face. I don't recognize the young man in the white coat who leans in beside her. Landon's loving eyes penetrate the fog of three months in a coma as she stares into my awakening. "I'm here, my love. I'm here to take care of you. I'm so glad you're back . . ."

I feel a tear skate across my cheek. I've never been so pleased to open my eyes. I look into the intenseness of Landon's face and I see hope. I can see a chance for new beginnings. I feel her soft touch as she strokes my arm and talks to me. She loves me . . .

THE ASHES OF SHANGIRL-LA

GENEVA NIXON

THERE IS AN island at the end of the world. Secluded, lost to everyone and everything. Its banks sparkle with sunsets and sunrises. Its waters bluer and deeper than the sky could hold. Trees blow there, pushed by the zephyrs that creep along their leaves. Streams flow inland from waterfalls upon cliffs. Dense vegetation surrounds pools for light game while insects roam about, busy bugs doing daily chores. The tide rises against its shores, then ebbs into the nestled ocean that is its home. This quiet world is Shangri-La itself; freedom was born here; peace was learned here.

Yet in this wondrous place, in such beauty that causes a star's envy, there is a woman who is not touched by the splendor around her. Her heavy heart is neither affected nor moved by her personal paradise, for what is paradise without love?

A storm has brought her here. Years ago a powerful disaster sent her vessel off course. Along with her was a lover. Waves crashed against the ship's hull, eventually splitting it in two. Down they all went, the woman, the lover, the ship . . .

"Icy memories. Please do me the honor and leave."

Day after day she watches the ocean. Food is plentiful and drinking water is abundant, though she hardly enjoys either. On the sand she sits with a photograph in her hand, eyes toward the water, toward longing, oblivious of the surrounding grandeur.

Once she was everything a woman should be: happy, charming, sophisticated, and passionate. Her body was sculpted, carved out of marble, the work of Michelangelo himself. Everyone who knew her loved her. Her brown-eyed gaze was one you didn't turn away from. Her mere presence lit up a room, the light radiating from her curling golden locks as her smile melted the wax on the candelabra. The damsel of damsels, with secrets kept deep within her bosom. Few knew this; few understood.

Except for one.

Dolphins in the distance sing songs of glee. Every now and then one shoots out of the water, flipping forward then back down. The surf clambers up against her feet, gently sliding over her toes. The only clothing she wears is what was salvaged from the boat: a pair of trousers accompanied by a dingy cotton blouse, both tattered and worn. Her hair hangs loosely against her back; the brilliant curls she once had are no more. Tears arise in her now-empty eyes as she stares at the sparkling waves, watching their never-ending movement, listening to their eternal cries. She grips the photo tightly, hearing the edges slightly crinkle. She glances down at it, circling her finger around the image of a face, that of a woman, dark and forbidden.

Not too long ago, there was a party. Rooms were filled with guests from all corners of the province. There was plenty of merrymaking here and there as deals were struck and handshakes were exchanged as pact makers. Gorgeous women, handsome men danced the night away, stealing kisses in front of onlookers surrounding the floor. Some even snuck away into shadowed corners, whispering dirty deeds that ensnared quivering loins.

But the Lady is nowhere to be seen. Up in her room she paces back and forth, her breasts slightly bobbing with her steps. Suddenly one of the windows opens and in climbs a young woman. Her skin is the Earth. The attire she wears is more to the liking of a man—fitted pants and boots with an opened shirt covered by a leather vest. Her hair is tied back with ribbon as strands fall against her face. However no amount of masculine attire could hide her gorgeous looks, her beauty unmistakable. Hurrying over to the other, they're immediately wrapped into each other's arms. Passionate kisses are given with tight embraces as the Lady begins to cry. The other stops for a moment to take her rouged face in her hands, smoothing her tears away.

"Why the tears? Tonight should be a time of rejoicing."

"I'm scared. At any moment we could be found and our plans ruined." She captures her in her arms again, as if holding on for dear life, her head lying against her chest, listening to the calm heartbeat that keeps her lover alive. "They could take you away, imprison you or banish me . . ."

"Shhh. Don't think about that. All the arrangements have been made. There's no way to halt what's to come. Fairly soon, *our* time will be at hand."

Looking at her sweetly the Lover receives a feverish kiss as her body is pulled against the other's, pressing her exalted breasts against her own. She can sense that her Lady is ripe. Collapsing in her arms the Lover walks her toward the bedroom door; pushed against it the Lady has no choice but to surrender. Hotter the two get, the Lover pressing her knee between her Lady's legs, kilning her desire. The Lover looks into her Lady's eyes, those unflinching deep eyes.

"Please, Emma. Say it to me," she implores.

Our Lady smiles back, kissing her lover in reassurance. "To the end of the world I'll go, anywhere to be with you. I have only my heart and nothing else to take with me, but all of it is yours until the sun and moon are one."

Deeper kisses and Emma receives them thankfully. Her Lover pulls up her dress, sliding her hand between her moist sex. Her emitting juices warm her Lover's fingers as she grips to her tighter, wanting her deeper inside every part of her ecstatic body. And she does just this as she pushes deeper into Emma, harder into her, taking her over entirely. Her Lady's body is bound in zeal, wanting only the woman in front of her. Wanting her to be a part of her every breath. And only her Lover's hands will do justice to her desires, only her kisses could ignite such prominent fires. Only her love could give purpose to this life.

Whispered words in Emma's ear, "I love you," then tears. Then organic euphoria.

Now tears again.

Night begins to mask the sky: time for a fire. After sparking the timber Emma settles in front of the flames. They dance toward the sky for her, reaching higher and higher. She marvels at them for a moment, enjoying their company. After a while she resigns to the cave that has become her shelter. The fire glows at the entrance of the cave, placing shadows behind her against the wall. Belongings from the ship along with wreckage that has washed up on shore are placed here and there on the floor: a splintered suitcase, barrels, lengths of rope, a shredded sail used as a curtain along with other meaningless things. And in the back corner, lying down on the mattress she made out of palms and clothing, Emma softly cries.

"I have tried, Jaiden. I have tried."

Her dreams take her back to her. Her Lover is there waiting every night. All hopelessness is lost at the sight of her; only love remains. Emma begs for Jaiden to make love to her, to push her into her rightful place, ensnared within her heart. And while Jaiden explores the depths of her, she in return explores Jaiden. But the dream changes and now they're both utterly naked, bathing in the inland pools on the island. Plumeria grows around them, sprouting from the enriched soil. Hibiscus and bird-of-paradise spring to life as well, busting about with arrays of colors and scents. Holding on to each other in the pool, Emma's back against her Lover's chest, droplets of water shed down her stomach, her hair. She leans her head back, opening her mouth to her Lover's tongue, letting it wrap around her own as she playfully kisses her. Jaiden's hands slide up and down her Lady's chest, feeling over her breasts then down between her soft thighs. Skillfully she takes her time tormenting Emma's skin. But suddenly phalaenopsis petals rain down on them, falling soundlessly on the water's surface. Emma places one of her Lover's hands over her heart while she leans back against her. Jaiden kisses her over and over again along her shoulders causing her to sigh in contentment.

"I'll never leave you," she breathes against her neck.

The day has come.

The sunrise creates sparkles on the ocean, millions of diamonds swaying side to side. Our Lady stands in front of this display, closing her eyes as she takes in the cool ocean air. Birds begin their morning conversations as the crashing waves roar against some unseen boulders. Tied to Emma's ankles are braids of rope attached to oversized rocks. She looks down at them, unsure of their promising purpose. Looking back out at the water she holds the picture tightly in her fist. For a moment she turns around and for the first time truly looks at her world.

"It's beautiful," she says softly, but then quickly adds while turning back to face the water, "too beautiful to bear alone."

Dragging her feet out into the surf she makes her way to deeper currents. Eventually the waves rush over her, and she doesn't come back up.

The island is as it was before, beaming with beauty unimaginable to you or me. And as the ebb runs out, a photograph is washed upon the sand. It's a picture of two women holding each other eternally close after much time spent apart.

WHITE SHOULDERS

JANET WILLIAMS

HER BLUE EYES, the lids now wrinkled at the corners, were as clear and cool as I remembered them. Fifty-one years had passed. I had not waited, and yet I always hoped this day would come.

◆

SHE WAS ESCORTED down the hall protected like a queen bee, the popular girls buzzing around all sides of her—Suzie in the front, Nancy with her fingers enlaced through the new girl's arm. They led her to locker 164 and stopped in front of me. Suzie rolled her eyes in the obligatory gesture I'd come to know.

"You share a locker," Suzie said apologetically to the new girl. "You'll just have to get used to it."

The new girl smiled sweetly. Her large blue eyes darted uncertainly between her new best friends and me.

"You can have the bottom cubby," I said, "unless you want the top."

Suzie clucked her tongue. "Of course she'll take the lower one. We don't call you 'Giraffe' for nothing."

"My name is Chris," I said, trying to sound casual. Heat poured into my cheeks and I stepped aside.

"I'm Inga."

Suzie hung up Inga's jacket. "C'mon. We have to get you to homeroom."

That was how we met.

Inga was not assigned to my homeroom. As I checked over my math assignment that morning, I thought about how the popular girls would get their claws into her. It wouldn't be long before Inga's innocent round eyes would turn haughty, a crime if ever there was one.

I saw her again in last period World Culture. Mrs. Hoffer walked her to the front of the room.

"Class, this is Inga Sorenson. Let's all make her feel welcome."

Inga waved timidly. She saw me and smiled a little. Even though I sat in the back row, there was no way she could miss me. I was a head taller than all the other girls. My mom told me everyone would catch up and we'd equal out one day, but that was just to make me feel better. Not too many girls topped six feet in their saddle shoes.

I liked seeing Inga at the locker, and I even made extra trips hoping she'd stop by to pick up a book or get her lunch. I never said much, just "Hi" or "See ya." She ate lunch at one of the popular tables, usually with Suzie who stuck to her like model airplane glue. Any day now I expected Inga would start rolling her eyes, having learned from the best. The only other time I saw Inga was in class—the back of her head mostly—but I didn't mind.

All that crap disappeared while I was shooting baskets on the court. It was the only time I felt like me. I used to play forward. Back in seventh grade, when I was new to the school, the kids cheered me on. A writer for the school paper called me a giraffe and the name stuck. That was a good year. They cheered for me, "G-I-R-A-F-F-E! Go-go Giraffe!" Four years later I was three inches taller. I hoped I was through growing. I felt like such a freak.

Other things changed in those last few years that pretty much stopped the cheering. The good news was I made the varsity team in high school. They put me up against the senior girls. My height was an advantage, but I didn't have the plays down like they did. I switched to guard and there was no reason to single me out. We made the division play-offs, but didn't take the trophy. I could live with that. I was thrilled our school had a team. The real problem was with Belinda, Nancy's older sister. Belinda was a good player and she took me under her wing. She helped me practice so I could be a forward again in senior year. She used to invite me to her house for a little one-on-one in the back driveway. One thing kind of led to another and instead of calling me "Giraffe," they called me "Lez." Talk turned to whispers and then no one had much to say to me. I only wanted to hit the books and practice my game. I figured if I tried hard, I could get a scholarship.

I thought I saw Inga in the bleachers during practice once, but when I looked again she wasn't there. It was probably some other kid. I saw Inga all the time in my imagination. I'd pretend we were walking down the hall together or holding hands on the bench at Percy Lane Park. I knew her perfume. I could smell it on her scarf. It made the whole locker smell like fresh flowers or breeze-freshened clean laundry.

She wasn't a bad student. I took a look at some of her papers—As and Bs mostly. Once I found a crumpled love note from Danny Barrett. I wasn't spying. It fell out of the locker onto the floor and I put it back. That's all.

You can imagine my joy when Mrs. Hoffer paired me up with her for our "Foods of the World" project. Inga and I pulled our desks together and talked about what we would do. She suggested we make her family recipe of limpa bread, a Swedish sweet rye bread. She could have said liver and onions and it would have sounded good to me. After class I played basketball and tore up the court.

A few days later she did watch me at practice after school. I changed into my Levi's and we walked the few blocks to her house. We needed to make a trial run of her recipe, even though Inga said she and her mom had made it a zillion times. On the way we talked about what it would be like to herd goats in the Kalahari every day of your life and never see a big city. In class we had seen a filmstrip about the Kalahari. The native people there are tall, too. I always sensed people were staring at me, but that day I wished they would. I wanted everyone to see me with her. I tried not to hunch over, an old habit I was trying to break. Inga was about five feet six—not a bad height. She had fair skin and pretty, long blonde hair that she braided and wrapped over her head from ear to ear like a headband. Some people did stare at us as they drove by, or maybe they were looking only at her. I would have. At her house she introduced me to her mom.

"It's nice to meet you, Mrs. Sorenson," I said.

"Chris, Inga tells me you're on the basketball team. How are you boys doing this year?"

I inhaled and bit my lip.

"Mom, Chris is a girl! It's the girl's team!"

"Oh my, I'm so sorry! Well, then, they must be doing well with you on their side. I better leave you two. Everything's in the kitchen." She turned and left.

"Ach! I'm so embarrassed!" Inga said after the sound of her mother's footsteps faded.

My ears felt as if they would burst into flames. "It's not the first time," I mumbled. "It's OK. Let's just do this."

Her tear-filled blue eyes begged for forgiveness. The lakes in Sweden were probably the same blue—cool and deep. I could have kissed her right then.

We put on aprons and she read the recipe out loud. I grated the orange peel and measured out the flour. If it had been me working alone, I'm sure I would have made a huge mess, but somehow everything came together and we cleaned up a little as we went along. She showed me how to knead the dough. That was my favorite part.

We played Monopoly while the bread rose. It took longer than I thought. Mrs. Sorenson invited me to eat with them and then went out of her way to tell Mr. Sorenson about the *girls'* varsity team. He nodded in approval. When we sat down to dinner, Inga's brother, John, came home. He was several inches taller than I and talked about being a senior, though I didn't recall seeing him at school. The rest of the evening went pretty well. I wanted to try the bread and I hung around until it cooled. It was great! John said it was better than usual. Everyone insisted I take half the loaf home to my family.

Inga and I spent the day together on Sunday and made our bread to take to school on Monday when our project would be due. Her brother searched the refrigerator for three or four things while we prepared our ingredients and he told me the secret to making lutefisk. I was glad we had decided on the limpa bread. The lutefisk sounded awful. The last thing I'd have wanted to do is bring fish to school. This time as the bread rose Inga and I stayed in her room and played music. She asked me what I thought about some of the boys, including Danny Barrett. I didn't have much to say about any of them. I had never been on a date.

"My mom says guys will ask me out in college," I told her. "I don't really care if they do or not."

"Of course they'll ask you out. They'd be stupid not to," she said. "If I were a boy, I'd ask you out."

"What?"

"I would," she said with an air of defiance. "It's important to get to know all kinds of people and do all kinds of things. You have to cultivate a well-rounded personality. The Suzie Klepermans of this world think they have it made, but they don't. She carries me around on her arm like I'm her newest handbag. It's insulting! She never studies, unless you call flirting a subject, and she's only interested in herself and what people think of her. Of course you want to look your best, but beauty fades. I think those popular girls are boring now. I can only imagine how dreadful they'll be in fifty years. Can I do your hair?"

"What? My hair?" I tried to keep up with the shift in conversation and Inga's unexpected comments, but I'm sure my bewilderment showed.

"I want to brush your hair."

Reflexively, I touched my short hair, wondering if there were more than a few strands out of place. "Sure."

She sat me at her dressing table and hummed a few times before placing her brush to my head. I felt the heat of her body and smelled her perfume as her wrists passed by my face. I discovered she wore White Shoulders from a visit to the department store where I smelled all the counter testers until I was positive I recognized the scent. The bottle sat on her dressing table. I knew that was it. I hoped some would cling to me as she moved around and let her sweater touch my shirt. Taking a deep breath, I closed my eyes and tried to record every movement as she tugged gently on a few snarls and played with my hairstyle.

The only other woman who had ever brushed my hair was my mother, although there were a few times when Belinda had run her fingers through it. Belinda disappeared after school ended, getting busy with a summer waitress job and then going away to college. I couldn't ask Nancy about her. It had taken the whole of summer vacation for things to die down and since that time I had not dared think about anyone else getting that close.

Inga and I got an A on our project. The kids loved the bread and by the end of class only crumbs remained on Inga's decorated bread plate. Danny Barrett and his class partner made Hungarian goulash. They spilled half of it on the floor. It smelled weird and the sauce had the consistency of mud.

Inga sat with me at lunch the next day. "They should have called that dish 'Hungarian galoshes' because we needed a pair after they spilled it! Could you believe it? Yuk!"

Inga laughed. "At least it tasted better than it smelled."

I ignored Suzie and Nancy staring at us from the popular table. "Good thing we didn't make lutefisk!" We crinkled our noses and laughed louder.

"My brother wants to ask you out."

I set down my milk carton and fiddled with the straw.

"He said he sees you walking in the hallway between second and third period."

"Yeah. I'm hard to miss."

"Chris! Don't say it like that. He wants you to go with him to the dance, and because you and I are friends he thought he should ask me first. It's OK with me."

"I don't know if that's a good idea." Her blue eyes looked sad and I felt like I was turning her down. I wished Inga could be my date. She was dear to me and now she was calling me her friend. "I've never been to a dance."

"I want you to be there!" she pleaded. "I'm going with Danny."

"I don't know."

"Come on. It won't be the same without you. Please?"

"What's the big deal? It's just a dance." I took a bite of my sandwich.

"It's the last dance before winter break and . . . we're moving again."

I stopped chewing and tried not to let my mouth drop open.

"My dad finished his job early and they're sending him back to St. Paul. My mom's packing up the house and we're leaving between semesters."

I swallowed hard. The half-chewed sandwich pushed at the pain in my throat. My eyes glassed over and I held my hand over them to hide my emotion. "You just got here! You said we could go to the park next weekend and . . . and . . . you already knew you were leaving!" The tears spilled onto my green plastic plate. I grabbed my tray and dumped everything into the bin on my way out of the lunchroom.

I managed to put that moment behind me because every moment of every day would be precious until she moved. For reasons I never completely understood, she wanted to be with me too. We did as many different things together as we could think to do. She came to my house and showed me how to mend tears and sew on buttons. We played records and she showed me how to dance. Even though I was taller, she pretended to be the boy so I would feel more confident dancing with her brother. It was hard to concentrate when our bodies touched. I took her to Percy Lane Park where we played Horse and practiced dribbling on the paved court behind the civic center. We sat close to one another on a bench so she could catch her breath and she let her hand rest on mine. It was very daring. Inga seemed brave about a lot of things, including her move back to St. Paul.

One day I heard Suzie ask Inga why she spent so much time with me. I walked up and glared at Suzie. I didn't want her to think it was anything like what happened with Belinda. Inga deserved better and I was beginning to think I deserved better too.

I walked Inga home after practice. I felt comfortable there. Her family was nice to me, especially John. Around their house I saw evidence of the change to come. Packing boxes stacked up in her living room, and the inevitable sank in a little more with each additional box.

On the night of the dance, John picked me up at my door. He pinned a carnation corsage on my dress and walked me to the car. Inga and Danny sat in the back. Danny looked good in his suit and tie, and I guess I could see why Inga thought he was OK. Inga looked like a princess. Her braid was set in place with rhinestone bobby pins and her corsage was banded to her wrist.

I watched her sway to the music on the dance floor and caught sight of her petticoats during fast numbers. The rhinestones sparkled in the light and I thought I could smell her perfume, even at a distance. John and I danced and thankfully I never tripped or stepped on his feet. We all took a break and the guys got us punch.

A few seniors I didn't know talked about a lowrider out in the parking lot. The guys went to check it out, but Inga and I decided to walk around. The school hallways were deserted and the classrooms were shut. We passed by our locker. Inga spun the combination and pulled out a small wrapped gift.

"It's for you," she said brightly. "Open it." Her tone was forced and I knew then she was as broken up as I about our parting. Our friendship had turned into something more.

I pulled out a small cloth sampler suitable for framing.

"I embroidered it myself," she said.

I smoothed out the creases against the face of the adjacent steel locker door and read: "Make new friends, keep the old, one is silver, the other gold." I felt a glow of warmth rush through my body. "Inga, it's beautiful! I'll cherish it always."

"See? In the corner I put my name and the year so you'll always remember me and the good times we had."

I scanned the hallway for students. Assured we were alone, I put my arms around her. "Inga, I will always remember you."

"Come with me," she said. She took my hand and headed toward a classroom. The door was locked. She quickly tried four more and let out a small shriek when one opened. She pulled me in and locked the door behind us.

"What are you doing?" I laughed.

We walked to the darkened back corner of the room. In the quiet I could hear the sound of our breathing against faint music from the gym. She held my hands and swayed to the rhythm a few times, then slipped her arms around my waist. I held her as we rocked side to side. Wispy hairs, fine as gossamer, tickled my nose and I smoothed them out across her temples. I lightly touched the tops of her white shoulders, her pearls, and felt the scoop of her dress collar.

I leaned in and kissed her forehead. She looked up at me and we kissed. For one sweet moment I was in heaven. The music changed to a faster beat, but we stood unmoving. I closed my eyes and held her close, feeling the pattern of her braid next to my face. I breathed in her perfume, letting it settle into a special place where I could hold the memory long after she moved away.

◆

"I WOULD HAVE recognized your eyes anywhere," I said to Inga. "You're still as beautiful as I remember."

"Oh, don't be silly! I'm a grandmother. I've got three kids, two boys and a girl, and five grandchildren. Did you . . . ?"

"My companion had a daughter before we met. She lives nearby."

"Your companion?"

"No, her daughter. My companion died six years ago. Breast cancer."

"Oh, I'm sorry." Inga touched my arm. "I wrote you," she said. "Maybe you didn't get my letters."

How could I tell her I had read those letters until the paper yellowed and wore through at the fold lines? "I wrote you, too. Dozens of letters," I said. She looked at me quizzically. "I never sent them. It wouldn't have been right. And you got married. Even though we had . . . feelings, I know you're not like me."

"No, not in that way." She sighed. "I've been fortunate. I've had a lot of love in my life."

"I didn't expect you here at our fiftieth reunion. You only attended our school one semester."

Inga glanced away and looked around the rented hall as if searching for one of our gray-haired classmates. "I contacted the reunion committee. They told me you were planning to come. I wanted to see you again. I'm fairly independent and enjoy short trips. My husband would rather not go anywhere until he gets his knee replaced, but you could visit us if you like. Old friends are hard to come by these days. Oh, crap! Here comes Suzie. There's no privacy at a reunion, is there?"

"Inga! Inga! It's you! It's me—Suzie Kleperman!" She sandwiched herself between us and I got a good look at her tightened face and unnaturally white teeth.

"Yes, just a moment, Suzie." Inga reached around for my hand and led me off a few steps. She didn't let go. She glanced back at Suzie and rolled her eyes. "Scary, isn't it?"

I grinned and held my laughter.

"Listen, Chris, if I write to you again, will you write me back?"

"Yes."

"Promise?" Her clear blue eyes shone beneath her sagging lids. Emotion swept through my body.

"Yes, I promise."

We quickly exchanged information and Suzie hustled Inga away to a group of once-familiar faces. I folded the piece of paper with Inga's address and tucked it into my wallet. I watched the crowd for a few more minutes, then finished my drink and headed out.

As I entered my house, I touched the glass over the framed sampler hanging in the foyer, the words faded from fifty years of sun. "Yes, I promise."

THE TRAIN RIDE HOME

ANGELA L. RECKLEIN

STANDING ON THE platform, Lauren could feel the vibration in her feet. The steel wheels made a high-pitched screeching noise as the train slowed to a stop. Clutching her bags, Lauren's hands began to tremble as she walked toward the other passengers waiting to board. Annie's phone call was so unexpected; it left little time to do more than throw some essentials in a bag, be sure to grab the black silk negligee that Annie had gotten for her, and drive to the train station.

Their parting two months before had been awful. Annie fell in love with Lauren and wasn't going to share her with anyone. What had started out to be a fantasy for Lauren's husband, Mark, had quickly turned into the destruction of the marriage. What is that old saying? "When you play with fire, you get burned." Lauren had feelings for Annie that she never knew were possible, especially with another woman.

On the surface, everyone would have a great time. Lauren wanted to experience making love to a woman, and Mark would have two women in bed. Annie wasn't so sure.

From the looks of it, the cars weren't crowded. After walking through two, the third one only had a few people; this would be perfect. Just as she lifted the bag to the rack above the seat, the conductor came by for the tickets. "Tickets please," he said. Fumbling for her purse, she took out her ticket. He stamped it and moved on to the next passenger.

Finally settled in the seat, Lauren let her mind drift back to their last meeting, one that she wouldn't soon forget. Annie played shortstop on a semipro softball team. There was a tournament going on, and she had asked Lauren to go.

"Lauren, have you got any plans for next weekend?" Annie said, hoping that Lauren would be free.

"None so far, Annie. Why?"

"I'm playing in a tournament down in Haynesville. Would you like to go?"

"Sure, it sounds like fun," Lauren said.

With a huge smile on her face, Annie said, "Pick you up at six-thirty Saturday morning. It will take us about an hour or so to get there."

Lauren was excited at the thought of going; it was something totally different. The rest of the week at work seemed to slowly drag by. Mark was out of town on business, so inviting Annie over for dinner on Friday night, would give them the chance to talk alone.

"Annie, why not come over to my place Friday night?"

"Will it be just the two of us, Lauren?"

Lauren smiled back at Annie. "Yes, as far as I know."

"See you then."

Friday, Lauren had finished all of her work and figured she would take off early, run to the store for a few things, and maybe even sneak a nap in. Her mind kept wandering about how attracted she was to this woman. An anxious feeling, mixed with an intense need to be with her. Just as well to go home early; she was preoccupied with thoughts about Annie. The rest of this work day was not going to be productive.

Traffic was light this time of the afternoon and that was a good thing; all the more time to get things ready for dinner. Driving down the street, Lauren wondered what she should wear. Pulling into the driveway, she glanced at her watch. There would be just enough time to put some things away, pick out what to wear for dinner, and get a few winks in.

With her head comfortable on the pillow, she drifted off and began to dream. The doorbell rang. As the door opened, Annie stepped in, and without a word, Lauren looked into her eyes, reached out with longing hands, and caressed Annie's ample breasts. With a surprised but pleased look on her face, she let out a moan to let Lauren know what her hands were doing was feeling especially good to her. She had this barely there sports bra and tank top on that showed off her golden tanned skin, glistening with tiny beads of sweat. Her tongue was aching to lick her. Her rock-hard nipples stood erect, nearly poking through the cotton material. Her voluptuous, muscular body seemed to be calling for Lauren's touch. The tattoos on her left shoulder were sexy as hell, and she knew it. Annie put her hand gently between Lauren's legs, and all Lauren could manage was a gasp.

Suddenly the phone was ringing—what an awful interruption! Lauren jolted off the couch, sending a glass of ice water flying off the coffee table. Instead of waiting until she caught her breath, still gasping, she answered the phone. "Hello?" she blurted in a disturbed tone.

"Lauren, it's me, Annie. Are you all right?"

While attempting to gain some composure, Lauren said, still not fully aware that her tone sounded so angry, "Sure, I'm fine, why?"

"Oh, just asking. You sound out of breath. I picked up the wine. Did you need anything else?"

Inside Lauren was thinking, *If she only knew.* "No, thanks anyway. See you soon."

After hanging up the phone, it occurred to Lauren how her voice must have sounded. Short, abrupt, and a little shocked. Annie was probably thinking, What the hell? Now back to clean up the spilled water. She grabbed a towel from the kitchen and patted the carpet dry.

How was she going to face Annie when she came over? What would she tell her about the phone call, the odd tone in her voice? No point in worrying about it. May as well start getting dinner ready and jump in the shower.

Stepping out of the shower, she reached for a towel. Rubbing it between her legs brought a wave of sensitivity over her still-swollen clit. That little dream had had more of an effect than she thought. Just then the doorbell rang.

"Hey, come on in, Annie," Lauren hollered down the hallway. "Just finishing my shower. Make yourself at home."

Annie came in and found her way to the kitchen. "I'm going to pour myself a glass of wine. Would you like some?"

"Sure, I'll be out in a few; the glasses are above the sink." Suddenly, Lauren was sure she heard footsteps coming down the hall. Before she could move, Annie slowly opened the bathroom door and held out her glass of wine.

"Here you are."

In Lauren's surprise, all she could do was hold her towel close and stand there, legs quivering. Annie playfully tugged at the towel and it dropped to the floor. She surveyed Lauren's body as though it were a fine piece of art. Leaning into her, Annie placed her strong hands around Lauren's hips and began to lick every last drop of water left on her skin. Lauren's breathing began to quicken as she moaned under the knowing skill of Annie's tongue. She had never allowed herself to feel such sweet abandon and wasn't sure what to do with it all. Annie was about to teach her.

"Annie, Annie, I can't do this. I don't know how," she whispered.

Annie looked up at her and said, "Yes you can, baby. Just relax and let me show you." Annie placed her hands on Lauren's shoulders and gently pushed her against the wall. As she pulled at Lauren's lips with her teeth, teasing her even further, Lauren's hands dropped to her sides. Annie's tongue went so deep in her mouth that Lauren's knees felt weak. Annie's hands trailed down, ever so slowly, circling her stiff nipples, pinching them lightly. Lauren took a deep breath and could smell Annie's sweet scent getting stronger by the minute. She started to beg Annie, "Please let me suck on your clit. I can't wait any longer."

Annie carefully parted Lauren's legs and pressed her hand against her mound of wetness. She slid one finger between her lips and began to rub her clit. "Oh, you're nice and wet for me, baby, aren't you?"

"Annie, don't stop—don't stop," Lauren pleaded. Right then with such a forceful thrust, her other handful of fingers were pumping in and out of her. "What do I do, what do I do," Lauren cried, as she rode her hand.

"Let it happen, honey. Just let yourself go." Annie felt the tightness around her fingertips, as Lauren's orgasm erupted. Annie held on to Lauren's hips and gently laid her face against her shaking stomach. Lauren looked down at Annie, and both of them just smiled.

Dinner was wonderful; in fact neither of them realized how good food could taste when it's shared with beautiful company. Conversation came easily, and the more they talked, the more they had to say.

Lauren said, "Would you believe it's already midnight?"

Annie laughed. "No way. Can it already be that late!"

"How about a snack, Annie? I'm starving."

They heated up some leftovers from dinner and gabbed throughout the night and into the morning. Adrenaline was coursing through both of them, so sleep wasn't necessary right now. There was silence as they looked out of the window and watched the sun rise. Neither of them could believe they shared so much and could feel this comfortable.

"What about your games, Annie? Won't you be too tired to play?" Caught up in each other, they never once considered that.

Annie snickered and said, "You worry too much, Lauren. Playing ball won't be a problem."

They packed up the car, filled the cooler, and were on the road at around six-thirty, just as planned. It turned out to be a beautiful day for a road trip. According to the weather forecast, it would be in the seventies, with a nice cool breeze out of the north. The sun was shining and it couldn't have been better if they had ordered it themselves.

When they got to the sports complex, Lauren looked around in awe. She had never been to a semipro softball game, much less a tournament with hundreds of people.

"I have to meet up with my team over at building C, and I want to introduce you to some of my friends," Annie said.

Lauren hesitated for a moment, and said, "Sounds good, let's go."

After a few hours of being there, Lauren realized how much of a good time she was having, watching all of these women compete. They were serious about the game and they were skilled at what they did. Watching Annie play was such a turn-on. She was confident, strong, and clearly loved her game. Oh, and it helped that in her uniform she looked blazing hot! This woman was blessed with curves that should be considered dangerous. While she was out on the field, every now and then, she would look up and give a smile and a naughty wink. She paid attention to her game and attention to Lauren. She made her feel special.

The weekend went by all too fast, as great times usually do. On the way home they laughed, talked over her games, and shared stories about the tournament.

"I had a great time, Annie. Thanks for inviting me to come along."

"You are welcome. I'm glad you came with me."

Things got pretty quiet after that because Lauren realized that it was back to reality, back to the mundane everyday of her straight, married life. It hit her hard that she hadn't been happy for some time now and that she wasn't in love with her husband. She had done what was expected of her. What she had done was settled. After having met Annie, getting to know her, the painful truth wouldn't leave her in peace. Lauren replayed it in her mind, making love to Annie. How natural it all felt. She tasted so good and she yearned for more. Nuzzled against those curves all night long, she knew in her heart she was home.

After unpacking the car, Annie glanced over at Lauren. "I'm not real sure how you're going to take this, but here goes. So much has gone on this weekend, and never in a million years did I expect this could happen. I can't leave here without telling you, Lauren, I love you." The words coming from Annie's mouth were exactly what Lauren was trying to deny.

"You need to give me some time to consume all of this, Annie. I can't just run off with you, and act as if I don't have a life with Mark." Everything had moved so rapidly, she felt as though her head were spinning. Some time alone to think, that would help. Her instincts were telling her time wasn't going to make a damn bit of difference. "Maybe some time apart will help us to put things into perspective," Lauren said.

Annie looked at her and said, "Nothing is going to change the way I feel about you."

The days seemed to drag on until the two women spoke on the phone each evening. They were never at a loss for conversation. Lauren struggled with being married and straight. She had wanted to turn and run from the altar the day she was married. That was all chalked up to wedding-day jitters. She knew then that she was a lesbian but couldn't admit it. She couldn't live the rest of her life not being true to herself; she had to do something. This wasn't fair to anyone, especially Mark. Things between them weren't OK, and they had fought many nights over it. The distance had become almost unbearable. When they were in bed, Lauren was repulsed when Mark tried to touch her.

The whole situation became unbearable for Annie too. One evening as Lauren was clearing off the dinner table, the phone rang. Lauren felt a sudden reluctance to answer it. It was Annie, telling her that she was going to be leaving town for a while, possibly stay with some relatives.

"Don't leave, Annie. Please," Lauren pleaded.

"I just can't stay here the way things are, Lauren. It hurts too much for me to pretend nothing has happened between us. And knowing you're there with him every night. You asked for time so you could make a decision and I've given you that."

Lauren was stunned. There was an awkward silence as though the phone had gone dead—a click, and she was gone.

Lauren never knew that something could hurt this badly. Pain was one thing; the reality of Annie leaving was a totally different thing. It was like someone had ripped her heart clear out of her chest. She sat huddled in the chair and began weeping inconsolably. Annie was her soul mate and she was letting her go.

Later on, trying desperately to gain some composure, Lauren picked up the phone to call work. She had to let them know she wouldn't be coming in the next morning. Mark walked into the room and stood at the doorway glaring at her. "I don't even want to know the details of that conversation. I'm flying out to Houston tomorrow to finish that job and should be back in a few days if everything goes as planned. When I get back, we'll talk." With that, he turned and left the room. Packing up his luggage, Mark reasoned with himself that if this were another man, he could compete, but not a damn woman.

The train came to an abrupt stop. Lauren jerked in her seat. Some crackling sounds came over the intercom and the conductor made some inaudible statement. Something about a delay and having to switch tracks. As if this trip hadn't taken long enough already. Lauren pictured Annie's face and beautiful eyes, reminding herself she would be seeing her in person very soon.

It wasn't long before Lauren knew that she didn't want to live her life without Annie being part of it. The fallout from this decision would be hell, but she couldn't imagine living a lie to make everyone else happy. Fumbling through the phone book, she searched for some of the phone numbers Annie had written. A few friends and several close relatives. Maybe she had called one of them? Lauren crossed her fingers and dialed. Surely she would have contacted her friend who played on her softball team.

Annie had indeed called her and Lauren wasn't at all prepared for the harsh response. "Lauren, don't you get it? Annie stayed here for a few days, and yes we talked about what has been going on. You need to leave her be and let her get over you." *Click* went the phone, and that was it; she had hung up. Lauren's heart sank.

At her wit's end, she figured there had to be another way of getting a hold of Annie, and she wasn't going to give up now. There was always e-mail, no matter where she was; she would still read those, right? Days went by and turned into weeks, but Lauren refused to give up hope. If they were meant to be together, one way or another, Annie would contact her. Please don't let it be too late.

A few days later, while Lauren was working at her desk, the phone rang. Probably a service representative calling with questions about their last order. Let it go to her answering service; she had enough to deal with that day. If it's important they will leave a message. Lauren pressed the speaker button just to be sure it wasn't anything major. "Lauren, it's me, Annie." She couldn't believe her own ears and quickly picked up the phone.

"Annie, Annie, I'm here, how are you?"

"I'm OK I guess. What about yourself?"

"Miserable without you here. Where are you?"

"I'm staying at my aunt's house in Indiana. I got your e-mail."

"Is there any possible way we can meet to talk?" Lauren asked with tears streaming down her cheeks.

"I'm in Chicago taking care of some business, and I leave to go back tomorrow morning."

Lauren had to think fast; she was going to see Annie, even if it was for one last time. She had to at least tell her that she had made her decision and wanted to share the rest of her life with her. They talked and figured it would be a good plan to meet in Chicago. Lauren could catch a train. After getting off the phone, Lauren's pulse was pounding. This was a chance to make it all right; the decision was made.

After what seemed like forever, the conductor announced that the train was pulling into Ogilvie Station. Lauren gathered her bags, jumped out of her seat, and stood by the doors. She was going to be one of the first passengers getting off of that train. The doors opened and she couldn't walk fast enough. Looking all over, amongst hundreds of rushing strangers, she didn't see any sign of Annie. Lauren's mind was racing. Maybe Annie was just in the washroom, or running a bit late. Then, looking over toward the big glass doors that led into the station, she spotted her. It was so wonderful to see her again.

Lauren, not caring about the crowds of people all around them, threw her arms around Annie and hugged her tightly. The hugs were OK; it was after the kiss they realized there was an audience. Neither of them cared. Words weren't necessary. What mattered was they were together, starting a new life. They had, after all, come home. Lauren and Annie would face life ahead, together.

SO MUCH TO DISCOVER

BETSY CONNOLLY

I FIRST MET Collette when we were freshmen at Boston College in 1975. A few days after starting school, I became fast friends with Collette's roommate, Diane. Having been active in youth groups at church for years, Diane and I met at a meeting about singing at Mass on Sundays. At BC, I lived in a different dorm than they did. At night I would trek across campus to hang out and practice with Diane. But she was always on the dorm floor's pay phone with her best friend from home, Jackie, who attended another college in Boston. While I waited for Diane, Collette would talk with me for a few minutes before heading out to catch up with her own friends.

Eventually, Collette started staying home and we would talk longer and longer. Our story starts here.

One night Collette hung around for what seemed like forever. "Aren't you going out tonight?" I asked her, wishing she would go. I didn't know her well. We weren't friends and I was a little intimidated by her; she ran with a more popular crowd.

"Well, I was, but I hate to leave you here by yourself."

"I'm OK," I replied. "I have my guitar with me so I can play and sing. That's what I always do after you leave."

"How long is Diane usually gone?" Collette asked.

I was a little embarrassed to tell her that I was sometimes alone there for hours, so I said, "Not too long."

"Well, it's already been more than half an hour tonight," Collette said, pausing. "That's a lot of quarters. I'll just wait here with you. I'm not interested in going out anyway."

"OK," I replied. She had no idea how many quarters Diane would need for her average call to Jackie. Collette and I sat in silence, a pregnant pause. I was so nervous that I couldn't think of anything to say.

"Why don't you play something for me?" Collette asked. She'd heard me play before but only with Diane, who always overshadowed me, definitely playing better. I played the guitar to accompany my singing; Diane sang and played well.

I was nervous about playing for Collette by myself, but I said, "All right."

I picked a Leonard Cohen song called "Suzanne," a song I played a lot. I sang and Collette quietly hummed the chorus with me:

And you want to travel with her
And you want to travel blind
And you think you'll maybe trust her
'Cause she's touched you
And she's moved you
And she's kind

I looked over at Collette who was lying back on her pillow with her hands behind her head. Her eyes were closed and she appeared to be really taking in the music. Skinny and sort of lanky, she looked like she was thirteen or fourteen. She was a little tomboyish and not particularly attractive—not my type at all. All I really knew about her was that she came from a big family and that she was studying to be a nurse. When she first told me about the nursing I wondered why she didn't want to be a doctor, but I didn't ask.

When I finished the song, she said, "Wow! That was great. Your voice is beautiful. Can you play more?"

I played my favorites until Diane came back. She barged in, making a real entrance like she always did. I stopped playing and singing and Collette sat up in her bed. For the first time I noticed how beautiful Collette's brown eyes were; maybe she was someone I could be interested in. Diane moved about the room tossing things around. She threw her shoes into the corner and tossed her leftover quarters onto the desk where they went everywhere. It was like she hadn't even noticed we were there. Her eyes were turned up and her jaw was clenched. After she hung up with Jackie she was usually gloomy and frustrated. She flopped down into the desk chair and looked at us.

"What's the matter?" I asked.

"Oh, I don't know. I talked with Jackie for hours and hours and we went around in circles, as usual. I don't know what I want from her but whatever it is, I'm not getting it."

"What's the problem?" Collette asked.

"If I knew that, I might have a solution," Diane replied. "I just know that I want her to be honest with me and she isn't."

"Did she lie to you again?" I asked. The day before Diane had told me she was sure that Jackie was lying to her. She'd said, "Jackie says she wants to see me, but then when I am there she ignores me, like I'm not there. She's obviously lying to me. She doesn't want anything to do with me."

"No, it's not that. It's too complicated to explain to you guys. Sorry. I just need to shut up. What're ya doing?" she asked.

"Well, Betsy was just playing some songs for me," Collette replied.

Diane leaned over, grabbed her guitar out of its case, and quickly launched into a verse of "Amie" by Pure Prairie League. She sang loudly, strumming with strong, hard rhythm, showing her anger and frustration. When she was finished she looked at me. "Do you wanna play together?"

I never had the oomph, the passion, behind me to play like Diane. I played more gently, more relaxed. But I said, "Sure," knowing she'd calm down so I could keep up with her. She always did. We played our usual songs while Collette continued to lie on the bed listening and occasionally humming along.

◆

AFTER THAT FIRST night, Collette and I didn't need Diane anymore. We would hang around by ourselves, talking and listening to music. Or I'd play my guitar and sing. Collette would lie on her bed while I played, like the first time. I'd sit on Diane's bed. Soon, Collette moved to the other end of Diane's bed, leaning against the wall. Over time, she slid closer and closer to me. I liked having her near me. I could smell her. While she didn't wear perfume, she had a distinctive Collette scent. It was a combination of a flowery shampoo or soap smell and light sweat, probably from not washing her clothes often enough. Soon she was close enough to touch me. If she liked a song, she'd lean over and put her hand on my leg where my guitar was perched, leaving it there until I stopped singing.

One night she leaned over and tentatively kissed me. It was a soft kiss on the very edge of the right side of my mouth.

Startled for a moment, I wondered if I'd just imagined it. I didn't know what to do. Before I could even say anything, she kissed me again, this time more fully. I kissed her back. Her lips were soft and tender, tasting sweet, kind of like warm milk with honey.

"You are a good kisser," Collette said, smiling.

"You are too. I can't believe you kissed me."

"Is that OK?" she asked hesitantly.

"Yes, I liked it. I'm just surprised, that's all," I replied. I was nervous and ecstatic at the same time. I'd wondered what it would feel like to kiss someone straight on the lips. Now I knew.

"You looked so nice sitting there singing. I decided to kiss you and see what you would do."

"Did I do what you wanted?" I asked, seeing her smile, hoping I'd done the right thing.

"You kissed me back!" she said, giving me a hug.

It was exam week so we had a lot of free time and we spent most of it together. Very little studying got done. A few days later, I'd be leaving for Illinois. I was going home for Christmas vacation and this parting was lingering over us. Eventually the last day came. Diane had already gone home so I stayed overnight with Collette. We spent most of the time saying good-bye, kissing, holding hands, lying on her bed, and relaxing with our arms and legs draped across each other.

It snowed a half a foot during the night. At dawn, there was still a dusting coming down. We plodded slowly through the snow carrying the heavy trunk to the corner where I was meeting a taxi to take me to the airport. I was sorry to be leaving Collette but I was eager to get home. It had been a long four months. I'd moved halfway across the country by myself, gotten through the first semester of college, made some friends, started an intense relationship with Collette, and I was beginning to discover my sexuality. I needed a break and some rest, physically and emotionally.

◆

WHEN WE CAME back in January, Collette started calling me "baby" or "doll" or "baby doll," when we were alone. I'd never been called any of these before and they seemed kind of childish for eighteen-year-olds. But I kind of liked being called doll. Without the baby part it was more adult-like, how men in the movies sometimes called their girl-friends doll. Before long I was calling Collette doll too.

Sometimes, I felt claustrophobic. I wasn't used to lying around so all the time, let alone being with one person day and night. But I also felt extremely desired and loved and I craved this. No one had ever wanted to be with me in this way. Sometimes I was deliriously happy, like our time together would just go on forever and ever. At these times it seemed like there was nothing to worry about.

On the other hand, for months, Collette and I moved back and forth, sometime panicking about what we were doing (and we hadn't even had sex yet), questioning whether our relationship was morally correct, but other times enjoying each other. The volatility of our emotions came and went on an hourly basis. Sometimes we would feel dirty, repulsed, disgusted, and ashamed of what we were doing. It was weird and kinky, abnormal. All around us girls were with boys, women were with men. They'd hold hands, kiss in public, and practically lie on top of each other on the grass by our dorm. This was normal. It was what we had learned from our parents, from church, books, television. Collette and I weren't normal. Sometimes when I was disgusted, I remembered how Collette really loved me and it felt wonderful. And then there were times when Collette was uncomfortable and I was so in love with her that I felt great. The worst was when we were both mortified by what we were doing. The best was when we both thought we were lucky to have found each other.

Once, we were hugging and kissing in an empty room in the dorm basement while doing our laundry. Across the room, in the shadows of one of the basement corners, someone walked by. We couldn't see who it was. Not knowing how to define it yet, we hadn't told anyone about our relationship. Now someone had seen us kissing.

Panicking, I said to Collette, "Did you see who that was?"

"No," she said. "Do you think they saw us?"

"They must have. They were looking right at us," I said, hoping I was wrong and that they had just walked by and not seen anything. They had been pretty far away.

"What if they tell people they saw us kissing? What if someone asks us about it, what should we say?" Collette asked me.

"How do I know what we should say?" I replied, irritated that I was supposed to have all the answers.

I was really worried. Should we tell people we were kissing? That was almost unthinkable. Should we let our friends and roommates find out from this other person who'd seen us? We ended up taking the path of least resistance, deciding to let people hear it from someone else—the easy way out. Admitting what we were doing to more than ourselves was not something we were ready to do. We were cowards. It never occurred to us that many people probably knew already. I'm sure this juicy information was not a secret for long in a dorm of a few hundred women. But no one ever said anything to us; no one said they saw us kissing.

✦

COLLETTE WANTED US to live together our sophomore year, but I wasn't ready for that type of a commitment. So when we came back in the fall, Collette lived off campus and I lived in a triple with two friends, Mary and Sue. It was almost like we were cohabitating anyway because Collette was over at our room multiple times a day; she was practically living with us. We (Mary, Sue, Collette, and me) set up our two connecting rooms using one room as a bedroom and the other as a sitting room. There was a single bed and bunk beds. Mary got the single bed (she was the first to arrive when we moved in). I had the bottom bunk and Sue had the top. From somewhere we obtained an extra mattress that we kept on the floor underneath my bed, for Collette, when she stayed over.

Collette and I made love for the first time that fall. It happened in my dorm room while my roommates were sleeping (at least I hoped they were; they never said they were awake). Sue and Mary had gone to bed hours before. Collette and I were hanging out in the sitting room. It got late, too late for Collette to safely walk back to her room off campus. I got in my bed and Collette pulled out the extra mattress and lay down on it. We had followed this routine many times so we both knew what to do.

But this time, after lying quietly for a few minutes, Collette sat up and put her hand underneath my T-shirt. She softly ran her fingers over one of my breasts. I closed my eyes and thought, I can't believe someone is *touching* my breasts. She couldn't reach the other one without coming up onto the bunk bed with me. While I was sort of in a surreal state of mind, I was aware enough to know that making love on the bottom bunk was likely to wake up Sue, who was on top. So I joined Collette on the mattress on the floor.

We kissed each other urgently (more of a sense of urgency than we usually did; our kisses were usually tender and loving). Her lips were softer than ever and moist. They tasted salty. We touched each other everywhere we could reach, trying to be quiet. Collette got on top of me and while she moved her body slowly over mine I couldn't believe how soft she was. It felt like I was rubbing cream over my own body, but this was someone else's body, another women's breasts, stomach, back, legs, neck—Collette's body. After we climaxed we lay still, frozen in time, for a few short moments, moments that went on forever.

After Collette fell asleep, I climbed up into my bunk so neither Sue nor Mary would wake up and find us together on the floor. I remember lying awake for some time sensing pangs of regret, disgust, and guilt, surmising, Oh my god, I really am a lesbian. Up until this point my knowledge of being gay was related to emotions, not actions. Now I'd actually had sex with another woman. I was afraid of what it meant and apprehensive about what the next day would bring.

The next morning we woke up and went about our day, like nothing had happened—no life-changing event. My fear stayed with me all day. Later, after dinner, Collette and I worked up enough nerve to talk about it.

"How are you?" she tentatively asked me.

"I'm OK, I guess," I replied, but I wasn't OK at all.

"Are you all right about what happened last night?"

"Well, I've had this nervous sensation in my stomach ever since." I was more anxious than when I sang a solo in the high school talent show.

"Do you think Sue or Mary heard anything?" she asked.

"I doubt it. They would have at least moved around to show us they were awake if they were."

"I guess."

"What'd you think?" I asked Collette.

"I can't believe it happened. I mean, it just happened. I just started touching you—" she stopped without finishing her sentence.

"Well, I don't want to do it again. Kissing is enough. Let's just leave it at that, all right?" I stated, taking a definitive stance.

"I guess," she said, sounding a little relieved and disappointed at the same time. Then she asked, "Can we still hold hands and lie on the bed sometimes?"

"Yes, but let's be careful about who's around when we touch each other. I don't want to be touching when other people are around." It was OK for the two of us to know about us, but I didn't want anyone else to find out.

I was blown away, anxious, and afraid. I don't remember experiencing any positive emotions after that initial feeling of bliss. Probably half my anxiety was because I had sex with Collette while Sue and Mary were sleeping right next to us. As if having sex with another woman wasn't deviant enough, we had to do it with two other people in the room. I wasn't a control freak but I usually was in command of my actions. This time I'd lost control. We decided it would never happen again, at least I did.

After this we kept it clean and went back to lying on the bed and to soft and tender kisses only. No significant touching and no sex. Collette liked having her back scratched and her legs and feet massaged for what sometimes seemed like hours. I never enjoyed this but I made a point to do it more often, an offering instead of sex.

Collette's room also had bunk beds and she had the top. When Lisa, Collette's roommate, was out, Collette and I would lie on the top bunk; I would try to study my intermediate accounting and she would read her nursing books. I hated accounting; I found it harder than anything else I'd ever studied. Sometimes when I didn't do well or just didn't get it, from Collette's bed, I would whip the book across the room and onto the floor (just like my father used to throw the lawn mower), saying, "Accounting is the stupidest subject."

Collette always knew when Lisa would be returning, but one day Lisa came home early. As her key went into the lock, forgetting we were on the top bunk, I pushed Collette off me. She flew through the air off the bunk.

Looking very startled to see Collette in midair, Lisa quickly asked her, "Are you OK?"

Trying her best to make a safe landing, Collette answered, "Yes, I'm fine." Then, standing up as straight as she could, she said, "You're home early."

"My study group ended early so I decided to come home and change before heading out to dinner. What have you guys been doing?"

"We're just studying too." Collette shrugged. "Who are you going to dinner with?"

Lisa launched into a long monologue about some problems she was having with her friends, issues that were impacting who she was going to meet for dinner. Lisa was always easy to distract. I continued to lie down on the bunk, listening. Collette put in a few words here and there. While they were talking, Lisa changed her clothes and then she left. Collette came back up with me.

Laughing, Collette said, "I can't believe you pushed me off the top bunk."

"I'm sorry," I told her. "Are you OK?"

"I'm fine. Just glad I have good balance."

"Lisa's so oblivious. I can't believe it. Nice job changing the subject." I'd been surprised at how easily Collette had changed the conversation over to Lisa's dinner plans.

"Yeah, you know Lisa. She always has some conflict going on. I wonder what she'd say if she knew about us."

"It's amazing to me she hasn't figured it out." I really was surprised. But I was certain Lisa didn't want to know anything.

◆

IN COLLETTE'S DORM there was an empty room because two people didn't return to school that fall. You could sign the room out for the night, day, whatever time frame you wanted. It wasn't authorized by the school, but no one stopped it. One day Collette signed the room out. We would, she told me, with privacy—no Sue or Mary or anyone else—spend some time alone together and see what happened.

Not fearing anyone's key in the lock, we relaxed like we'd never done before. For a long time we just lay on the bed, a single bottom bunk bed. We didn't need music, alcohol, drugs, or anything; being together without worrying about being barged in on was enough. Collette unbuttoned my shirt. She took hers off. Softly we touched each other's breasts and kissed each other on the lips. Then Collette gave me soft, little kisses all over my face and down my neck until she was leaning over me, kissing my breasts and my stomach. I kept pulling her back up to me so I could look at her. I wanted her to continue kissing me but I wanted to see her too. She helped me take my shirt off altogether and then she unbuttoned my jeans and pulled them off. She slowly moved her hands all around over my underpants, on top and underneath. Then she put her hands inside and started to massage me.

I stopped her and said, "Wait a minute, I want to touch you too," and I started to unbutton her pants. She pulled them off and stripped completely naked. Then she climbed on top of me.

Again, I stopped her. "Slow down, let's just lie here for a minute and relax." I wanted to relish the moment and turn it into hours, not be rushed.

"I really love you," she said softly, as she kissed me tenderly on the side of my lips.

"I love you too." I kissed her back.

We lay there, naked, uncovered, on the bed, for a long time. I had wrapped my arms around the back of her neck, holding her, taking care of her, and pulling her into me. She lay on her side with her body close to me, her arm draped over my breasts. Every once in a while one of us would lean in and kiss the other gently. Then we'd hold each other's face and kiss more urgently and deeply.

Eventually we touched each other and climaxed. The closeness of it, the kisses, touching, sex, and saying we loved each other, blew me away. What a contrast to the disgust and guilt I'd felt the first time.

Afterward we continued to lie there for a long time, holding each other, cuddling, and saying "I love you" more, until Collette said, "I'm hungry. Want to get something to eat?"

"Sure, I guess," I replied, without a lot of conviction or energy; hunger wasn't even close to being on my mind. I could have stayed there forever. But Collette got up, so I did too. Sitting up, I was dizzy and lightheaded. Maybe I sat up too quickly; maybe it was love.

We got our clothes on, picked up the room a bit, and headed off to the dining hall for dinner.

After that day, we used the room as often as we could.

◆

COLETTE AND I stayed a couple until 2004. We had many happy years together, but eventually we decided it was time to separate and pursue other, separate dreams. The most precious outcome from our twenty-five-year relationship is that we have three children, now twenty, sixteen, and nine.

TWO-WAY LOVE STORY (HER COUCH IS WIDE)

NICKI REED

WHAT DAY DID I give her my heart? What date? I think it was a Tuesday. I know it was afternoon. All of my classes were in the afternoon.

Was it that first day? The first time I saw her *wow!* dressed in black: black hat, black glasses, her sense of humor matching. Was it then? I know I sat up straighter.

Or was it when we had our first lesson the week after?

Her hair in plaits, her big black boots on, she told us about herself *yes, gorgeous, but what do you do at night?* then she asked about us. I tried to be just me, just another student, but she got it out of me. I'm a mother.

She liked that. Another mother with another son.

Weeks later we had our class trip to the state library. My teacher strode in from nowhere and made camp on my toes *please don't stand so close to me.* I stepped back a little and she leaned in closer, her hair catching in my mouth. I pushed the hair out with my tongue *mmmm, what else can I get a taste of?*

We took the guided tour, me close behind my teacher *hope she forgets about books and leads us somewhere dark and warm and lonely* and not listening to a damn thing the librarian said. After the tour, we sat in our scholarly group and went over the coming assignment for the hundredth time.

When I stood up to leave, my teacher stood up too.

"Going my way?" she asked.

"Yes," I said, "yes, I am." *Whatever way that might be. I'll put my commitment on ice, and go straight to hell in your bed if you like.*

My quick trip home became bent out of shape, an unkempt circle.

We made our way to her little red car, trading six-year-old-son stories. I liked her dark-eyed honesty and self-deprecating style and the little sidelong glances I was taking into her buttoned-up shirt *how about we get that off, at speed, buttons flinging, ping, ping, ping.* In her car, the windows up, hot sweat lining my upper lip and sides of my nose, I soaked up the warm brush of her knuckles every time they bumped my knee on their angled sweep from first gear to second, third, fourth, and back again.

She pulled over for me just after the big, wide intersection that signalled our separate ways. I watched her little red car speed off, the tram tracks glistening silver. Smiling for no reason, I drove home on the freeway, the fast black road to my partner, to my child, to my mortgage. I parked in the garage, went through my heavy front door and up the twenty-two steps to my real life.

◆

PARTNER, WHEN I look into your blue eyes, the same color as mine, I'm not sure I love you anymore. The longer I look, the longer I wonder. I see myself in the twin reflections of your pupils and I don't think I want you. I'm growing out of you.

But I keep it together for our child and our mortgage.

Speaking of our mortgage, I think I love our mortgage more than you. I love the overbearing size of it and I love the weight of it on my shoulders. My mortgage keeps me honest, keeps me where I'm meant to be. When I said we could be three, I meant it; when I said forever, I meant it.

Here is where I'm meant to be.

But I'm not here.

Not in my head.

And lately I haven't been here in my heart either. I don't think you've noticed. You're wrapped up in your work; you're all about the things we can afford now; you're comfortable in the idea of the old, silent me.

So tonight I say my hellos and how was your days, and I make my right noises, give my correct responses, the whole time thinking about her worker's hands, her poor driving, her raucous laugh, and her ripe, wide mouth.

Tuesday afternoon can't come fast enough.

◆

I'VE ENROLLED IN another class with her, Wednesday nights, five til nine. I've got an industrial-strength interest in my teacher *it's nothing a two-hour fuck on the floor of her office wouldn't fix.* I'm a mature-age student with a mature-age crush that is maturing nicely, thank you very much. I'm twenty years younger with a willing body and a filthy mind. I don't mind where my mind takes me *as long as it's with her, as long as she wears that orange top that shows the welcome slash of skin at the midriff, as long as she wears that perfume, the sweet, cheap-smelling one, along her chin, down her neck, and deep down into her décolletage, I don't mind.*

It's bodily. I say her name; my heart skips. I see it written, again, and again, and again, in heavy blue biro in the back of my book; my heart stops. The smooth, rounded vowels of her confident, mature voice make me nervous, skittery, unpredictable. I think about getting my hot and itching hands on her all day long, from breakfast to dinner. And through the junk food in between.

And I write about her. When I'm at home with my mortgage, I make my edits and my rewrites. I detail it all in Times New Roman, and I delete it too. My mortgage need never know. Detail. Delete. Detail. Delete.

◆

PARTNER, I HAVEN'T had butterflies in my stomach over you for years. They've flown away. We got too safe, too comfortable, the air got stale. Butterflies need fresh air, a twist of winter, an autumn breeze to leaf through. I can't remember the excitement of knowing your phone number, the tremor of your early kisses, the discovery of our first nights with each other. I can't seem to care about your hands and face and tongue and tits anymore. Not today.

Perhaps I'm being unfair, perhaps I could try harder. Maybe I could get there again, in my mind at least, if I could remember it. Are you there? Do you remember it, tshe falling in love? Is that what we did? Does the memory keep you going? Is a good memory all I need?

I don't want to recall our first kiss.

I want to make a memory of a new first kiss.

◆

WEDNESDAY NIGHT AND all I want to know is who the fuck sits like that?

Women don't normally sit with their legs wide open. It's very suggestive. I've got it and you will see it, *yes let's, how about the ladies' toilets on level two?* and it's very inviting; I've got it, would you like some? *why yes, yes I would. I'll start at the top and work my way down.*

It's making me wet. It's making my night.

I sit back in my chair and take in those strong, long thighs, in tight dark denim, heavy stitching running up her legs, down her pelvis, all of it meeting, X marks the spot, at her cunt, and I chew my lip.

I've put my hand up to my forehead so I can shield my eyes. I don't want the whole class to see me staring into that splendid spread. *That's right, babe, open them just a little more.*

My cunt is on fire, there's no better way of saying it. It's a soggy, swollen heat. For a moment I consider going to the toilet and relieving the pressure—it'd only take a minute. I think about my fingers inside me and twist a little in my chair. *God, I need to come.* I decide against leaving the room because I can't miss a minute of this. I blow out a sigh, cross my legs, and wait it out.

The class finishes. My teacher and I pack up together and for no good reason she drives me to my car. I'm parked out the front of the building, just like the week before, and the week before that, but she drives me round to my car, just like the week before, and the week before that.

We sit in her car, squashed against each other *see how much space I can take up if the need arises* and talk. I can smell my cunt, warm, wet, and delicious, and I wonder if she can smell me too *how would my cunt taste from your lips, babe, shall we try it? Right here?* I'm not listening. I'm thinking about her squashy back seat and her wide-open legs.

It's late and we say good-bye, the click of her car door closing seems to echo extra in the empty car park. I drive home, my pants sticky. She must know what she is doing to me. She must. She must know what I want to do to her. She must.

TONIGHT I RUN up the twenty-two steps super quick. I don't think about my mortgage, not once.

I wrap my arms around you and you're surprised.

"I need you, babe."

I haven't called you babe in such a long time. I'm calling you babe, because in my head, on paper, out loud in private, I call her babe.

You like my attention but you play hard to get. You try to pretend that you've got a say in this, but you haven't, not tonight. We get to bed and you're on your stomach pretending to be asleep until I climb on top of you and push my pelvic bone hard into your back.

We roll into each other and kiss, our tongues rolling, sliding. It's nice to kiss you again, like this, like lovers, even though in my mind you're not you, you're her.

When we come apart you lower your head and it's her hot, full mouth on one of my nipples. I can practically feel her thick, long hair bunched up in my fist. You suck my nipple in time with our pushing and pulling and then you've got a hand between my legs. You softly, slowly, rub my clit.

It's not enough.

This thing started hours ago and I need to finish it. I grab your hand and shove your fingers hard and deep into my cunt. Twisting, probing, pushing inside me are her fingers. They're experienced, motivated, and they know me already.

My stomach makes an oozy flip, my scalp tingles in a multidirectional swirl, my spine becomes electric, a circuit board of unruly sequenced flashes and sparks, and my cunt swells and bursts. It's begun.

TWO-WAY LOVE STORY (HER COUCH IS WIDE)

◆

ALL THIS TALKING in my teacher's car, in her office, on her couch, online, is adding up to something. Holding her when she cried while pushing my nasty, inappropriate thoughts to the back of my mind, having her laugh at my jokes, press my arm, check me out when she thinks I'm not looking *It's the T-shirt. It's tight and it makes my tits look positively edible (if only I could reach) and it makes my stomach look flat and taut (I did say "look")* is adding up to something.

It's becoming bad maths. Addition of the complicated kind. It's turning my harmless lust *who cares, not me, just get your gear off, babe* into dangerous love *people could get hurt, or worse, I could.* I think that I've started to care *shit.* I think that I love my teacher.

I think it is time to tell her the good news.

I can't do this on my own anymore.

I'll put out a press release.

I'll bang up a billboard.

I'll wack it on the whiteboard on Wednesday night.

I'll tell the most indiscreet person I know so that it gets around like Paris Hilton on Oscar night and my teacher can come to me for a correction.

I'll stop being stupid, ridiculous, immature. I'll get a grip *that's what you do in these situations, isn't it?* and I'll tell her.

My teacher can do with it what she will.

She can reject me if she likes *after I fuck her;* she can kick me out of school *right after I fuck her;* she can even tell me she's straight *but right after I fuck her.*

PARTNER, HAVE YOU ever loved two people at once?

I have. I love two people right now, today.

I realized this in the shower this morning. My hands in my hair, thick foam squelching through my fingers, I was thinking about my next assignment, then my teacher and then you. And that's when I knew that I love two people.

I love you like I always have. Predictable. Settled, comfortable, and a little bored, but here where I'm meant to be. Forever.

And, Partner, I love my teacher. I don't even know her, not really. Does she run away from a fight? Will she race me for the car keys like you do? Or does she stay to the finish? Like we should. I'd like to find out.

I can do it. I can love two people at once.

I'll do the everyday love thing with you, we can be safe and the same, and I'll do the wild, heart racing, mad-sex thing with her.

I can do it. I can love two people at once. It'll be easy.

◆

THESE ARE THE SYMPTOMS.
Enjoy them at your Leisure.

When she walks into the room, through the mint green door, and you know she's about to come through it, because you were watching and waiting for the door handle to move, and there, it just did, here she comes, it makes you catch your breath. Every single time.

When she calls you, her number lit on your phone, your fingers tremble as they try to press the little, tiny, too-small green button, the button minute and unmanageable, and tremble, try, tremble, try, you answer it.

When you see her little red car in the car park, and the light on in her office, and your silly heart leaps jubilantly out of your chest, cartwheeling across the asphalt, until you tell it to get the hell back in and compose itself.

And when she laughs, you do.

When she cries, you do.

When she breathes, you do.

I'm going to tell her tonight. I've planned it. Plan is as follows: Drive to her place. Knock on her door. Give her the flimsy pretext I've invented for being there *have toothbrush in my back pocket for successful outcome and have hip flask of something alcoholic in glove box for otherwise*. Tell her.

I'm sitting across from her on her black leather couch, the couch I dreamt about two nights ago *why do I always wake up just as her lips hove into view?* the couch I daydreamed about over breakfast this morning *I can get so much closer when I'm actually awake* and I'm going to tell her.

We've been talking for a couple of minutes and I haven't found a point where it's just "come up." I'm going to have to make it come up *tell her*. I'm getting turned on looking at her bare feet *tell her*. I'm thinking about her feet sliding up and down my calf *tell her* and it's distracting me. I'm giving myself a pep talk *just tell her!* while I make pretty with conversation.

OK, I'm telling her

"My sister made a bet with me." *you're not*

"A bet?" my teacher asks, confused.

Of course she's confused. Without taking a breath I've leapt off onto some tangent, the angle sharp and ridiculous.

"Yeah, she bet me five dollars I wouldn't tell you something *oh, god, you are* so, anyway, do you wanna run away with me?" *pathetic*.

I say it fast. I spit it out. I swear it lands on the floor I'm so quick.

She catches it. She's got it in her hand and she's looking at it, turning it this way, that way, then she looks at me, her dark eyes serious, her mouth smiling.

"Have you got a crush on me?"

"Just a tiny little one." *liar.*

She gets up off her chair. I watch her cross the room toward me. I watch her sit down next to me and put her arms around me. She kisses me on the cheek, and we sit there, our cheeks touching. She says something.

"I've got a crush on you too. Just a tiny little one." *so not only do we have a common interest in books and film, we have telling lies in common also.*

"I thought so." *do something.*

We hold each other and all the bravado I've had in my head for more than a semester is gone. Her couch is wide and long and I'm thinking, *now what?*

And then I remember her bare feet, her hands, and the way she sits; my cunt twitches and my bravado is back.

"I'm going to kiss you now." *are you going to announce everything tonight? I sure hope not.* The leather couch squeaks.

I kiss her very, very softly on the lips.

It's a tentative kiss, our first kiss. We're cautious, feeling our way, the way you do when you're in an unfamiliar room in the dark, a touch here, a slight move there. I suck on her bottom lip, she sends her tongue in, her own careful exploration. I suck in an excited breath, hers and mine. I push hard into her, putting my tits into hers and a knee between her legs. She moans and pushes back, sending her satin, silk, felt, velvet cushions to the floor.

I think we kiss for an hour but it may have been a minute.

Then things happen quick, like carpet burn. Like clothes-flying, fast-moving movie sex. Like the scene in the '80s TV series *Moonlighting* where Dave and Maddie finally do it and the coffee table lands on its side. Like when you're in a big, big hurry, in case someone phones, or someone comes in, or someone comes to their senses. Like there's too much clothing between you and your objective and you never do see your purple sock, the one from France, again.

She tells me this is her first time with a woman though she's thought about it since forever. I say, "You'll be fine, I love you." *why did you say that?* I get her out of her clothes and I get out of mine. She tells me that she's scared and I tell her, "Don't be, I love you." *it's too early to say that.* I slide down her body. She tells me that she's going to come, she yells, "Don't stop, don't stop." She whispers my name, over and over and over *it is the best thing I have ever heard,* and her hands in my hair, my mouth on her cunt, two fingers inside her, she comes.

I come up from between her legs and she pulls me forward and kisses me; our tits squash together deliciously *you said it.* Her arms around me, her mouth on mine, I wonder what will happen next and I wonder where my control of the whole thing has gone *you said it.* She turns us over and she's on top of me *you said it;* she's put her hip into my cunt and she's making good progress on the orgasm with her name on it that I've had since mid-semester.

We grind our hips.

The top of her leg is hard into me. Her solid thigh is wreaking havoc on my clit. There's sweat on my stomach. She's kissing my neck. I grab her ass. I pull at her. I'm going to come. I'm squeezing her hard. So hard I'm probably leaving bruises. But I don't care.

And then she's on the edge too; she's stopped kissing me; her chin's going to put a dent in my collarbone if she keeps this up and her hair is in my eyes, my nose, my mouth. She's banging away at me like it might be the last thing she'll ever do.

I come. She comes. Our voices loud in her silent flat. And then I do the last thing I expect. I cry *like an athlete on the podium my medal gleaming gold around my neck*. I burst into tears *like someone who's lost something incredible because they said I love you too early*. And she kisses my tears away; we sit up and she holds me, her arms around mine, my back leaning into her warm, large breasts. We sit on her couch and say nothing. Just sit.

◆

PARTNER, IT'S NOT that easy and it's not that neat.
I know that. One night, one fuck, and I know that.
I love her and I love you.
Why have you become more interesting all of a sudden? Could you sense I was leaving, in my head at least, and now you're bringing your A game? Is that what you're doing? I like it, but it's unnerving me.
I love you and I love her. And I told her too soon. I told her all of it; I was planning to hold onto it, keep it safe, and now she knows.
She's got control.
She's got the keys to this thing.
She's got one set and you've got the other.

◆

MY HANDS IN the sink, my eyes fixed out the kitchen window, my suburb is leering at me *in love with two women at once, idiot* the undulating hills domestic, dressed in houses, driveways, mortgages, mock me *nobody can make two women at once work, idiot.*

I leave suburbia behind and daydream that I'm not in my kitchen that I'm back in hers. I'm pouring us wine, then padding barefoot across her ancient thready rug, back to her and her couch, and handing her her glass, holding on to mine. I sit in my spot, between her legs, our calves resting against each other, my feet small against hers and I'm swirling the ruby liquor round and round, slow, clockwise. I look into that liquid spiral, take a breath, and gulp it down. It travels harsh down my throat and settles in my restless stomach.

I'm back. I'm drying the dishes, I'm sweeping the towel across the plates, around the cups, into the bowls, and I'm trying to think of nothing but manual labor. Wipe, wash, rinse. I've vacuumed twice and mopped once. I plan to do the bathrooms next. Wipe, wash, rinse.

But distraction isn't working.

Her black leather couch is the only place I want to be.

My phone rings. It's her. She wants me to come round. She wants to "talk." She's going to let it go before it's begun. I know it.

On her couch we sit tight together; she's holding my hand; she has just finished kissing the tips of my fingers *god, please don't. If this is over, then please don't,* and it looks like she may have been crying. But she isn't crying now because she has something to say.

She details the reasons why.

"You're in a committed relationship."

she's right.

"You're too young for me."

she's right.

"You're my student."

she's right.

"We could never go public."

what would your mother say?
"We'd fail spectacularly anyway."
we will if you expect us to.
"You're in too deep. You're smart and funny and very attractive, and I really, really like you." She sighs, shifts her weight.

For half a second I consider asking for one last fuck *that mouth, those tits, her couch, my indestructible immaturity.* But I care too much about her to be that gross, that out of the moment, I respect her too much. I leave it.

And she is so, so right.

"You'd better go home now."

I'm already standing up; I've got my bag slung over my shoulder; I've got my keys in my hand. She catches me up at her front door, touches my hand one last time, hurriedly turns her face into her shoulder. I don't see her shut the door behind me, I only hear the heavy thud resonate up the driveway.

◆

PARTNER, I'VE BEEN shopping. Retail therapy is as good as chocolate. I've spent a lot of money, but it's fine, we can just put it on the mortgage.

I've made a few changes around the home.

So what do you think?

You like it don't you? You've always wanted a black leather couch. I was the holdout. But I've changed my mind.

And the rug, do you like the rug? I do, but I think it'll look better in a couple of years when the bold, twisting colors have faded, and the threads have become wide, loose, and ragged.

I sit on the couch, pat the spot next to me, and push the cushions out of the way. I look up at you.

"Come sit next to me, babe."

I HEART YOU

KISSA STARLING

TEDDIE SLIPPED THE list in her pocket, picked up the phone, and dialed the resort to confirm her reservation.

"Seven o'clock tonight, that's right. And you'll have lilies on the table by the bed?"

"Yes, ma'am. And we'll save the table next to the fireplace as you requested. Your room key will be under the place mat at dinner. On behalf of all of the staff here at the Magnolia Inn, I'd like to thank you for choosing our establishment for your love nest needs every February fourteenth."

There was a slight chuckle on the other end of the phone. Teddie and Bea had a personal relationship with most of the small staff at the mountain getaway.

"You're quite welcome, Murray. And enough of that laughing. Bea and I wouldn't think of going anywhere else. If it ain't broke, don't fix it, right?"

"Yes of course, ma'am. I happen to think you're our cutest couple!"

Reconfirming the reservation was a moot point, but Teddie did it every year regardless. Others clamored to get a weekend at the now-famous resort, but Teddie and Bea were among the select few whose reservation stayed on the books. Attendance at that very first Valentine's weekend in 1979 guaranteed them a yearly spot.

The side door by the garage opened and shut. "I'm home."

Teddie smiled and shed her clothing as she spoke. "It's about time. I can't believe you had to go in today of all days. Get in here, woman."

Bea rushed through the door, eyes wide. "You're naked!"

"And you're not. What's the problem? Ahh, you must have forgotten where you were. Go back and look at the sign on the door."

"Teddie."

"I mean it. Go look."

"I don't have to walk across the room to see your silly Love Shack sign. It's a good thing we don't have many people walking through our bedroom door."

Bea sat on the edge of the bed, flipped open her computer, and clicked on the icon to open her e-mail. Teddie moved closer. "Open that one."

Bea found the indicated e-mail and clicked. A huge heart appeared.

"I wrote you a love letter."

"I see that." Teddie read over her shoulder.

You mean more to me each year we're together. I look forward to making year #31 our best yet!

It was signed, *I heart you.*

"Enough of that, babe. Close that thing and come here." Teddie pulled Bea toward her. Bea closed her laptop and threw her purse to the floor. She stood up right in front of the floor-to-ceiling mirror. Her hips swayed back and forth while her hands cupped her slightly sagging breasts. First she unzipped her black trouser pants and let them fall to the floor. She stepped out of those and picked them up with the pointy toe of her black flat. Teddie laughed out loud when the pants landed in a corner.

"Take it off, baby."

The mirror reflected her backside and a sheer thong that barely covered her shaven mound. Her fingers unbuttoned the cashmere shirt with just enough pause to make Teddie yell, "Get on with it, bitch."

Bea wiggled her ass and held the fabric up away from her shoulders. With a turn of her head she twisted around, dropped the shirt to the floor, and kicked it back against the bed skirt. Lace surrounded the top of her cleavage. Her nipples poked through the seam. She reached behind her back and unhooked the skimpy brassiere.

"You're killing me here. Hump me now or lose me forever." Bea smiled at the reference to their favorite movie, *Top Gun*.

Her palms flattened her breasts, holding the bra in place. The thin material slipped to the floor and Bea struck a pose with her ass against the glass of the mirror and her arms positioned above her.

"Stay right there. Don't move an inch."

Teddie stood up and sauntered over until there were only inches of space between them. She used her hands to touch the air centimeters from Bea's spotted skin. The anticipation caused Bea's tits to jut forward and her thighs to spread. Her engorged clit peeked from beneath her hood.

"I love how you open up for me. Turn your feet out and bend your knees." Bea complied with a lustful look in her eyes.

"Now tell me what you want. The more detail I get the more satisfaction you earn."

Only a few seconds passed before Bea spoke. "Get on your knees in front of me. I want your mouth right in front of my hot, wet, tunnel of love."

"Where in the world did you hear that phrase? 'Tunnel of love'? Have you been watching that European lesbian soap opera again?"

"Enough of that, Teddie. You're supposed to be following *my* directions, remember?"

Teddie knelt down and situated her lips in front of the sweet musky mons that contained the sweetest of nectars. She inhaled deeply. "Mmm."

"Good. Now grab me by the ass and stick out your tongue. In fact, swirl it around in circles and I'll do the rest."

Tasty vaginal juices churned around in Teddie's mouth, overpowering her senses. Bea humped up and down while Teddie let her teeth rest on Bea's swollen clit.

"I didn't ask for that you devilish imp!"

"Ahh, but you did want it, didn't you?"

Bea pushed Teddie down on the floor and mounted her mouth. "Eat this, baby." Teddie pushed against Bea's clit with her tongue. "Yesss. Don't stop. Please don't stop." When she bit down on Bea's outer lip her lover came, all over her face. The two women collapsed into a sixty-nine position on the carpet.

"I love you," Bea murmured against Teddie's cheek.

"And I you too, love," Teddie responded. They fell asleep with their pinkies intertwined.

◆

"OH, BLOODY HELL. Bea, wake up. It's six thirty. We've got to get on the road. Our reservation is for seven o'clock."

"Babe. We've been late for our anniversary dinner for

the last twenty-nine years. Why would you, or they, expect us to be on time for number thirty?"

"True enough, but let's get going anyways."

"Only if I can take this wine with me." Bea leaned over and pulled an entire bottle of Château de Brau Cabard Cuvée Exquise, Languedoc Roussillon 2003, organic of course, from her purse.

"What is that? I've ordered wine to be delivered to our room at the resort."

"I'll have you know that they age this in new oak casks to give it a lovely vanilla quality. I happen to enjoy the blend of Merlot, Grenache, Syrah, and Cabernet Sauvignon."

"You read that off of a box, didn't you?"

They laughed together as they lugged the suitcases out to the car.

"Well, maybe I did."

The car held warmth that the outside lacked. Teddie drove and embraced Bea's hand at the same time. "I Walk the Line," by Johnny Cash played on the radio. Thirty minutes into the drive, Bea started to sing along with the tune. Teddie joined in and they sang in unison up until they reached the Magnolia Inn.

A valet walked up and opened the door to escort Bea to the door. "I'll make sure your luggage gets upstairs, ma'am."

A second valet opened Teddie's door, stood back, and waited for her to exit. "And I'll park your car."

"Thank you, Henry, and thank you to you also, Sevin."

Teddie tipped each man as she walked around the car to clutch Bea's arm in hers.

"Off we go to celebrate thirty years of endless love, my dear. As usual I have a spectacular evening planned and maybe even a surprise."

"Oh, tell me please."

"All in good time."

"Well, maybe I have a surprise or two of my own." Bea flipped her shoulder-length brown hair and walked toward the door.

The oil lights burned low in the restaurant. Shadows filled every corner. Hand-holding couples sat at every table save one closest to the fireplace. That was their spot.

"Ahh, Ms. Reynolds and Ms. Wyatt. So glad to see you. Right this way." They stepped, hand in hand, following behind the maître d' until at last they reached their table.

Teddie sat farther from the fire. "I know how cold you get these days, hon."

Bea smiled and sat next to the spitting flames. "I absolutely love this place." Tears slid down her wrinkled cheek.

"No, babe. No tears tonight. It's our anniversary."

"They're tears of joy. Who knew we'd be together for thirty joyous years?" Bea reached for her hand.

Teddie reached into her pocket and retrieved the yellowed paper they'd both contributed to for so many years. The list held their hopes and dreams, their fears and worries—it even held their promises to one another.

"Is that what I think it is?" Bea's eyes wandered to the aged paper and then straight to the fire.

"Yes. I wondered if you'd remember."

"Of course I remember that silly twenty questions game you stretched out over the course of twenty years of anniversaries. A few of those questions came close to ending our relationship."

"But in the end each one made our commitment stronger. At least that's how I see it."

"And why did you bring them here tonight of all nights?

Why must we relive the daunting journey that made us what we now are?" Bea turned away to gaze into the fire. "I guess you remember why we stopped?"

"Of course I do. You threatened to walk out if we ever did it again."

"And I haven't changed my mind about that course of action."

"Do you trust me?" No response spurred Teddie to move over to sit upon the hearth. She rested her hands on Bea's plump knees. "Look at me, dear. I need for you to say that you trust me."

"I . . . trust you."

"Good. Now listen to me. I'm not doing this to hurt you or to cause you grief. I think it's important for us to relive the misery we were able to overcome. We've lived and loved for thirty years. I need for all the cards to be on the table here."

Bea continued to stare at the flames. Teddie moved back to her chair and unfolded the list.

She read just loud enough for Bea to hear. "Nineteen seventy-nine. Did you have sex with anyone else this year?" The waiter approached with the potato skins that Teddie had ordered ahead of time. Both women remained silent until he left.

Teddie took one small bite and waited for Bea to speak. "I almost left you that night. It was our first anniversary and I find out you fucked Betty Herndon three times. God help me I didn't bat an eye when she died last year."

"Bea . . ."

"I'm not proud of it but she took something from me

and it's taken me years to get it back. You were mine. She knew it and she still fucked you."

"It was always you I wanted. I was young and stupid. I never made that mistake again. Here, you pick a year to read."

She handed over the list and sipped from the water glass in front of her. Bea trailed her finger down the list and stopped halfway down.

"Nineteen eighty. Name one thing you spent money on that your lover knows nothing about."

"I knew you'd pick a year where you messed up. See what I mean, baby. Even as mad as you still are that I slept with that slut Betty you're still worried about the fact that most of these indiscretions are mine. Most of the slip-ups and idiotic happenings were my fault."

"I sent money to that Save the Children's Fund even after we agreed we didn't have the extra money to do it."

"You did. We ate beans and cornbread at least once a week for months. I was furious with you at the time because I didn't know why. Looking back, it's just another reason I fell in love with you. I'm the self-serving one."

Bea picked the list back up and touched yet another year. "Nineteen ninety. Who did you vote for?"

"That was a fairly easy year for us. We didn't argue at all that I remember."

"Only because I lied and told you I voted for the same man as you. I didn't. I actually voted for the Democrat that year. It was part of my rebellious stage."

Teddie laughed. "Well good for you. I never meant to stifle your thoughts, baby. I'm a little miffed that you lied but I understand why you did. Back then I would have blown up and maybe even left over something so stupid."

"I knew that. Hence the reason for my lie."

"Nineteen ninety-five. Which family member doesn't know that you're a lesbian?"

"I felt so bad that year. You thought it was a reflection on our love that I wouldn't tell my mother we weren't just roommates. My mother died not knowing how much I love you."

"I still don't understand that but that's one of the things I've learned. We don't have to agree on everything. I respect your decisions."

Bea handed over the list. "Your turn."

Teddie took the list and stopped on 1999. *Tell your lover a fantasy that you haven't been able to act out.* "This was the year I thought we were over. My fantasy involved multiple women with lots of Jell-O shots and you with a strap-on. Your fantasy was to get married and have kids. You met Ronald that year. I believe you even went on a few dates."

"It didn't mean anything, hon. At the time it was important to me. I wanted the white picket fence and the dog too. In the end I realized that you were all that mattered. I couldn't give you up if I tried."

"You always were the smart one. The list doesn't matter. What matters is that we got past all of that and still loved with all our hearts." Teddie bent down on one knee.

"And now that lesbian marriage is legal I want to make you my wife. Bea Wyatt, will you do me the honor of becoming my other half? My partner-for-life? My lover and nagger forever and more?"

Tears gushed down Bea's cheeks and onto her sleeve when she tried to rub them away.

"Yes. Of course I'll marry you. But there's just one thing . . ."

Teddie scooted her chair over next to Bea's and they

squeezed one another close. She slipped a diamond engagement ring on her beloved's finger.

"You've made me the happiest woman alive. And by the way, I heart you. Now what is your one thing?"

Bea plucked a velvet box from her pocket. "I won't be kneeling because I'll never be able to get up. Teddie Reynolds, I love you more than words can say. I can't imagine spending my life with anyone else. And I came to this anniversary table with ring in hand to ask you to be my wife."

Teddie's eyes grew wide. "You mean . . . we came here with the same intention? Oh my goodness."

"You silly, foolish woman—you beat me to the punch. Now, for the rest of our lives I'll have to hear about how you proposed first."

"You'd better believe it, hon. Now give me *my* ring before I have to jerk it away."

"Only after I say I heart you more. I even had it engraved on the back of your ring."

Bea fit the Celtic knot onto her future wife's left ring finger.

"Oh, baby. You remembered."

"How you always wanted a pewter Celtic knot instead of a diamond? Of course I did. As long as I'm able you'll always get exactly what you want—along with all that you need."

One woman rose and the other leaned down. Their lips met in the middle and touched lightly. Teddie placed her hand on the back of Bea's head and drew her closer. She thrust her tongue in and explored her lover's mouth. It tasted of mints and wine. When she pulled away the whole restaurant cheered. Bea looked away, her face red and flushed. Teddie sat back down in her seat. She captured her fiancee's eyes and stared into them. *I could sit and look into her eyes for days,* she thought. *Her soul is right there at the surface.* The waiter approached with their entrees.

"Could you bag that up and send it to our room?" Teddie looked to her love for agreement and received a head nod. *Good enough for me.* She took the diamond-adorned hand and led Bea toward the stairs. On the way she crumbled up the list and threw it into the fire. Bea rubbed the back of her hand and whispered, "Thank you."

"Last one up is paying for the wedding!" Teddie shuffled toward the elevator and held it open for her future wife. They held hands on the trip up to the room. Not a word was said in the hallway. Teddie slipped the key into the lock and turned.

"Wait. I want to carry you over the threshold."

"We aren't married yet."

"I know but I need the practice!"

Teddie heaved Bea up into her arms and carried her two feet before letting her slip onto her own feet. The door shut and Teddie watched to see how Bea would react. "It's beautiful. The lilies by the bed are the perfect touch. Now let's order porn!"

"You always keep me on my toes, luv. And I hope that's one thing that never changes."

"I feel the same way."

"Glad to hear that, Bea. There's one more thing I need to tell you before I lay down and watch *Suki Does Saturn.* You're such a nut with those lesbian sci-fi thrillers. Here."

Teddie handed Bea a thick notebook.

"What's this? Can't I look at it tomorrow?"

"We really need to call Shalya back tonight."

"OK, you've got me. Who is Shalya?"

"The lady at the adoption agency. One call and we go to the top of the list. There's a pregnant teen who's ready to deliver any minute."

"You mean . . ."

"Babe, I always wanted you to have your fantasy. I just had to make sure it was me you wanted to live with in that house with the white picket fence. Oh, and we're going to the pound tomorrow to adopt a dog too."

Bea's makeup smeared all over her face. She repeatedly wiped away the tears that slipped from her eyelids.

"Aren't you happy, baby?"

Bea smiled up at Teddie. "These are tears of joy. I never thought this moment would come. I always knew you were the one. I'm sorry that it took you this long to know how I felt."

Teddie walked two steps and grabbed Bea's body to hers. "No worries. It's you and me and that darn fantasy of yours forever. Just one thing though."

"Yes?"

"I'm still waiting for my fantasy. The honeymoon could be a good time to surprise me!"

Laughter spilled into the room. Teddie held Bea's head to her bosom. "That's it, baby. Your laughter fills my soul. It's no wonder that I heart you—more." She quickly covered Bea's mouth with hers and suppressed any one-upmanship from the future Mrs. Reynolds.

STEPPING OUT

J W HARNISCH

TAYLOR FOLLOWED A well-dressed older couple through the entrance of the fusion restaurant. The door opened and violin music poured outside. Taylor seated herself at a small table near the dance floor. The mellow atmosphere and dim lighting matched her mood. Give me somewhere to hide, she thought. She smiled over at the violin quartet, enjoying the Beethoven piece they played. An older waiter with a dark, slicked-back '50s ducktail approached Taylor's table with a bottle of red wine wrapped in a towel.

"A glass for you, madame?" he offered. Taylor accepted a glass and sipped appreciatively. She sighed. It had been a very long week full of too many compromises in her business and personal life. She polished off her wine and waved down the white-jacketed waiter. The waiter poured her another as two women were escorted to the booth opposite Taylor's table.

Taylor recognized one of the women as Cynthia Nokes, the well-known political talk show host. She had always seemed oddly familiar. She wore her dark red hair short and spiked, an Armani business suit and a guy tie, and spoke with a thick Brooklyn accent. Taylor was surprised at how petite Nokes was in person, although she bristled with energy. The other woman was about half her age, taller, and obviously her assistant. She carried an oversized pad of paper and a Mont Blanc pen. She placed two stacks of paper on the table with a deep sigh and alternated biting the end of her pen with passionate flurries of serious discussion with Cynthia Nokes.

Their waitress minced over to the table. She had a fake smile and a fake laugh. Unfortunately, she also blocked Taylor's view. Taylor craned her neck, trying to watch Cynthia, who was a newly out-of-the-closet lesbian. Cynthia hadn't noticed Taylor . . . yet.

"Hi! So, how are you girls this evening?" asked the waitress, her dark eyes excited.

"Ladies," Cynthia replied, correcting their waitress, who simpered awkwardly at the comment.

"My name's Shannon," the waitress said, her smile hitting full wattage again. "I'll be serving you tonight."

Cynthia looked up. "Shannon or Shawna?" she asked the waitress.

Taylor giggled, sipping her wine.

"Shannon," replied the waitress, controlling her irritation.

"Shannon," confirmed Cynthia.

"Shannon," repeated the assistant.

Cynthia gave her a look, but Shannon gave the blonde assistant a wide smile and a long look under dark lashes. Then she said, "Can I interest you 'ladies' in a cold beer, iced tea, two-for-one margaritas?"

Cynthia's assistant put her hand up to her mouth and made a little moue with her lips. "A beer?" she said. "Two-for-one margaritas? Why not just hand me a nuclear bomb! You'll have to call the cops on me!" She giggled at her own joke.

"She's a recovering alcoholic," Cynthia explained. Shannon tried nodding sympathetically, but only succeeded in looking a bit like a marionette.

"I am," the gofer said, "and my name's Janice. Hi!"

"Mmm, hi! yourself, Janice," Shannon said, giving her first real smile and a wink.

"Hi!" Janice said back, practically glowing.

"Anyway," Cynthia finally spoke up, looking annoyed at not being the center of attention. "I'll have a very dry martini, three olives, Grey Goose."

"All right! You go, girl," exclaimed Shannon. Cynthia Nokes looked at her with the strangest of smiles.

"Coke," said Janice.

Shannon smiled at Janice just a moment too long. Cynthia glanced sideways at Janice and Shannon, the tip of her pink tongue just showing, thoughts obviously churning.

Shannon winked at Janice before turning away to walk to another table.

"What the fuck!" Cynthia exclaimed to Janice. Her hands moved a lot when she talked. Taylor noticed and giggled, beginning to feel a little giddy from her wine. The quartet was packing up and another band setting up. A busboy came over with glasses of water for the women in the booth.

Taylor studied Cynthia Nokes, noting the gracefulness of her long fingers as she gestured. The new band started up. They were good, designed to get the dinner and bar guests dancing. Two drinks later, Taylor smiled to herself, and started an internal countdown. It's gonna happen, she thought. Sure enough, Cynthia's hand waved a little too close to her drink, and it flew into the air. The clear, cold liquid splashed across the parquet floor and all over Taylor's lovely legs and perfect pink pedicure. Her beige miniskirt was just long enough to be legal, and she froze as the icy drops splashed up her thighs.

"Oh!" she cried, involuntarily flinching.

Cynthia's eyes darted toward Taylor, then took a long walk up and down her bare, wet legs. "Oh! I'm so sorry—" Cynthia's contrite smile was suddenly wide and inviting. She hurried across the aisle with her dinner napkin. She knelt at Taylor's feet and gently stroked the napkin along one smoothly tanned leg.

"Don't you dare!" Taylor cried.

She sounded so familiar. "What did you say?" Cynthia asked, staring up into Taylor's big, leaf green eyes.

Their gaze locked, and Taylor suddenly gasped.

"Taylor Berillo?" Taylor nodded, uncharacteristically speechless. "I'm Cindy, remember?" she said.

Taylor was nodding and laughing in disbelief. "Cindy!" she cried.

Cynthia grabbed onto Taylor's knees. Taylor's green eyes widened.

"Taylor! Oh, I love this," Cynthia said, delighted. "After all these years. My god, you look fantastic! A little martini and olives here and there, but even that looks tasty on you!"

Taylor laughed. "You look great too, Cindy." They embraced, and soon the hug was a cuddle. Janice raised one eyebrow, then dipped a finger in the spilled martini on the table and sucked it off.

"Mmm, mmm! Fellow 'Closet Cunt'!" Cynthia giggled.

"No, 'Bullet Bitch.'" Taylor told her. "That's what they call me now." She smiled suggestively, still stroking Cindy's soft hand, and staring down into her velvety brown eyes. Cynthia admired her beautiful smile.

"Bullet Bitch?" she asked.

"Mmm-hmm, because I like guns so much . . . ever had your naked, hot body stroked all over with a smooth, cold pistol? It's heavenly." Taylor grinned.

Their hands caressed one another's arms, waists, hips.

"Mind if I join you?" Cynthia coyly asked her old friend. Her old clubmate. Her old crush from high school. But they had never actually hooked up back then. Taylor always had a boyfriend.

"What about your friend?" Taylor eyed Janice at the next table.

"Oh, Janice." Cynthia glanced over dismissively. "We were just talking business, but we're done. Janice, I believe it's a wrap. I'll see you tomorrow."

"OK, Cynthia. See you tomorrow," Janice replied, a knowing little grin touching her lips. She gathered up their notes, then called for the passing waiter. "Check, please."

Cynthia took the seat opposite Taylor. "Are you expecting anyone?" she asked.

"Just my husband."

Cynthia's mouth made a little *O*. Taylor grinned wickedly. "I'm only kidding."

Cynthia breathed a sigh of relief. The waiter arrived with more drinks and they ordered dinner. The music was flowing and people were starting to dance.

"It's been a long time, Taylor," Cynthia said, her naked foot stroking Taylor's legs under the table. Taylor smiled and allowed the caress.

"Yeah. You left for New York that summer."

Cindy smiled distantly. "I went up to Ithaca to study journalism. Wanted to do criminal justice, but . . ." Cindy looked down.

"But what?" Taylor asked.

"I wanted to carry a gun, and there were a few problems."

Taylor bit her lip, and Cindy stared at her mouth. "Guns," Taylor said, licking her lips. "How fucking sexy of you to want a gun!" Cindy sipped her martini, then licked her lips, unaware of the power she suddenly had over Taylor.

The food arrived, and each of the girls took a shrimp and silently tongued it, staring into each other's eyes. Then Taylor plucked a soft, round oyster from its shell, dipped it in butter, and slid it between Cindy's willing lips. Cindy returned the gesture, her fingers sliding inside Taylor's luscious mouth. She already knew what she wanted to taste. . . .

"Mmmm," Cindy sighed, and continued to lightly tease Taylor's lips.

"You know," Taylor grinned, "I kept the tradition going. I started a Closet Cunt secret society in college too."

"You did? How wild," Cindy winked.

"It was much wilder, in fact." They giggled and shared sly smiles.

Suddenly, Cindy leaned across the table and planted a kiss on Taylor's lips. It was sensuous and soft, and a little moist.

"Relax," Cindy whispered at Taylor's gasp of surprise. "Maybe it's time to step out of the 'closet.'" She picked up a wine glass, putting it to Taylor's lips, and then filled her own mouth with warm, sweet wine. She leaned over, and fed it and her tongue to Taylor.

A little while later, several empty wine glasses sat on the table. Their chairs now side by side, Cindy and Taylor sat thigh to thigh, Cindy's head on Taylor's shoulder. She lazily licked Taylor's earlobe.

The waiter approached the table. "Another drink, madame?" he asked Taylor.

"I've always wanted you, Cindy," Taylor told her, turning to stare deeply into her eyes, ignoring the waiter. Taylor ran her finger lightly across Cindy's lips, down her throat, and into her bra. The waiter watched silently, avid interest on his face.

Finally, Cindy turned to the waiter. "Would you bring me a dry martini? Make it very dry, with four olives, please."

Taylor said she'd have the same.

"Two very dry martinis, ladies." He stepped away, grinning.

"What brings you back to L.A., Cindy?"

"They're giving me a key to the city. You know, hometown girl makes good, and all that stuff," she gave a deprecatory wave. The band started another song. "Listen," Cindy said. "You hear that?"

Taylor nodded and smiled, then swayed slowly in her chair to the beat. The song was "The Way We Were." Taylor's green eyes brightened. They both had liked this song, years ago. Cindy noticed Taylor's big smile and grinned. She reached for Taylor's hand and pulled her up.

"Let's dance!" Cindy said, already wrapping her arms around Taylor's slim waist and gazing up into her face. She ran her fingers through Taylor's sleek blonde hair, then across her smooth shoulders.

They danced along the edge of the dance floor. The other patrons watched with wide smiles. Taylor's eyes were half closed. She felt Cindy's lips on her own, sweetly, briefly, then her tongue flicking. Taylor enjoyed the sensation, eyes still closed, feeling Cindy's hands slide across her back and over her hips. Cindy's hands cupped her tight butt and pulled her in close. Taylor gasped at the unexpected strength in Cindy's arms and body, vibrating like a live wire against her own, except for those softest places that felt hot and exciting.

Taylor thought back to when she'd craved doing all this with Cindy, but hadn't dared. Former Closet Cunts stepping out of the closet after all these years. Closet nothing, Taylor giggled. Everything was out in the open, finally.

The song ended but Cindy and Taylor continued dancing. Cindy kissed Taylor on the cheek but kept her lips pressed up against her smooth skin until Taylor turned her lips down to meet Cindy's. Tongues slid in and out, soft against soft, eagerness born from years of waiting overtaking shyness. The band was playing a new song, but the women didn't notice until another pair of dancers stumbled drunkenly into them. The dance floor was suddenly full of excited dancers, and they were jostled again. Taylor took Cindy's hand and led her back to their table.

"I would sooo love a little more privacy. . . ." She smiled suggestively. Cindy's breath caught in her throat at the sheer loveliness of the tall blonde eager for her touch and tongue.

"Let's go," Cindy said, her voice a low purr, her panties already wet.

When they stepped out the front entrance, it was raining lightly. Cindy offered Taylor a handful of peppermints she'd grabbed inside.

"I didn't know it was raining," Taylor said.

"Well, we were inside."

Taylor was too tipsy to feel dumb. Cindy laughed a little. "Mmm, yeah. I so want to be inside . . . of you," Taylor said, and giggled, running a hand lightly over Cindy's jutting nipples.

Cindy grabbed her hand and kissed it, then licked her palm. Then Cindy put her arm around Taylor's waist and walked her to the Lexus SUV in the parking lot. One of Taylor's tires was flat as a rail.

"Ah, I don't believe this! They're brand new," Taylor sighed.

"I'll change it for you," Cindy offered.

"That's sweet of you, but it's raining."

"I don't mind. I'm already wet." She grinned. "Hell, I've been wet for a while, now!" Cindy laughed, looking up at Taylor with a lascivious smirk.

Taylor shook her head and smiled. "You haven't changed. Always on top of things. Always in charge. Always exuding sex . . . yum!" Taylor said flirtatiously.

"Why don't I just give you a ride home?" Cindy suggested, running her hand up inside Taylor's beige miniskirt. "You can have that flat fixed in the morning." Taylor leaned back against the car, enjoying the caress. Her hips gave a tiny undulation. "Mmm, oh! Let's go," Taylor breathed into her ear.

They moved toward Cindy's ride and Taylor stumbled. Cindy caught her. "Maybe you did have too much," she said.

Taylor looked at her, a gleam in her dilated eyes. "Or maybe just enough," she giggled, putting her tongue out and licking Cindy's left nipple through her now damp and translucent pale blue blouse. Cindy pushed her nipple hard into Taylor's mouth. Taylor's lips opened invitingly.

They got in the car, and Cindy's hands were on Taylor's skirt, yanking it over her hips and exposing the pink silk string bikini beneath. There was a darker pink wetness up the center. Taylor laid her head against the charcoal gray leather upholstery. Her head was spinning, she noticed, as she let Cindy's hands pull aside her panties and push her long, golden thighs apart.

Taylor felt warm breath on her thighs, and a hard nipple graze her hand. She cupped Cindy's firm little breast, her fingers moving as if with a mind of their own, while Cindy's fingers pushed between her cheeks into her tight little ass, and a practiced tongue and more fingers pushed between her engorged nether lips.

Taylor's body started to move by itself, a gentle bucking and writhing, when suddenly—nothing. Taylor blinked to see Cindy idly stroking her fingers in and out, around and up, holding her pussy lips open while she smiled and watched.

"Cindy, for god's sake! Don't stop—" Taylor said urgently.

Cindy's eyes traveled slowly up Taylor's sleek body until they locked on her eyes.

"Oh, Taylor, I've been waiting so long to lick this pussy, it's just not gonna go that fast! Oh, no . . ." She grinned lasciviously and began to unbutton Taylor's black silky blouse slowly, button by button. Cindy exposed her matching pink silk lace bra, then pulled Taylor's big, pale natural breasts out, marveling that Taylor let her! Cindy's mouth clamped down tight over one dark nipple, licking and sucking, while her hand squeezed and flicked and played with the other. Taylor's head fell back again.

"Oh! But honey, here in the parking lot?" Taylor moaned.

Cindy grinned. "It's an old fantasy of mine from our clubhouse days, that you'd become my own little cunt. . . . Oh baby, you are mine tonight." Cindy mouthed and licked and squeezed. Taylor gave in to the hot, sweet moment as Cindy put her thumb on her clitoris and finger in her pussy. "I'll just play for a while," Cindy crooned in her ear. "Then we'll live another of my fantasies."

Taylor felt so oddly out of control, helpless, unable to stop Cindy from doing and saying anything she wanted, and more, didn't want it to stop. Her mind boggled—she always wanted control! Taylor remembered when she was twelve years old and wanted this very woman, girl then, to lick her, suck, fuck, and please her more than she would admit even to herself. I feel helpless and I love it! she thought.

A few minutes later, Taylor's moans were loud in her own ears, hoarse and begging. But again, just as suddenly, Cindy stopped. She sat back in the driver's seat, looking cool and collected, if a little breathless, smiling like a Cheshire puss. Taylor stared at her.

"C'mon, baby! Please—"

Cindy shushed Taylor by slipping a sticky wet finger between her lips, in and out, in and out. When Taylor tried to cover herself, Cindy shook her head no.

"Oh no. I want your panties off that gorgeous pussy, and those lovely titties where I can look and play with them all the way home. Do you understand me, Taylor?"

Taylor's eyes widened in surprise. Her reddened lips curved upward and she nodded, pulling her thighs apart even further and leaning over to rub her naked breasts against Cindy's arm. Her efforts were rewarded by skilled fingers pinching and pulling and probing. When Cindy next stopped touching her and started up the car, Taylor felt like she understood the game. While Cindy drove, Taylor reached between Cindy's legs, and then for her pert breasts, but was firmly pushed away.

"No! You must wait now, my pretty little pussy," Cindy leered at her then laughed with a throaty growl, betraying her own barely controlled excitement. Cindy's right hand kept pulling Taylor's pussy open wider, her fingers sliding wetly in and out at stoplights, pinching her now-red nipples at every opportunity. Only one passing motorist noticed Taylor's gorgeously naked breasts in the darkened car, and both girls giggled wildly as he nearly ran into a telephone pole.

They drove fast through the rain along Sunset Boulevard. "Third house on the right," Taylor said, her voice breathy and low. She found the remote in her purse and pressed the button. The garage opened and Cindy drove in.

"Want to come inside?" Taylor whispered.

"We are inside," Cindy responded, her eyes already half closed with longing. The garage door closed behind them. Cindy cut the motor and turned to stare longingly at Taylor, who returned the gaze. Both girls smiled. The garage was darkened and quiet; the only sounds those of the cooling engine ticking and their own excited breathing.

Cindy leaned in for a kiss. Taylor still had her legs apart, showing pink on the gray leather seat. She put her arm around Cindy's shoulders and her hand between her legs. Cindy's kisses were hot and wet all around Taylor's mouth, lips, and neck. Taylor's fingers sank deep into Cindy's naturally red curls, finding the wetness and sliding up and down, in and around, until Cindy's slight bucking movements finally belied her tightly controlled facade. Taylor smiled and eyed her with a serpent's longing, leaf green eyes turning dark with excitement. Cindy finally thrust her fingers inside Taylor's hot, wet pussy and moaned with delight.

"Mmm, oh Taylor! I always knew it would be this good . . . why'd we wait?" Cindy's left hand finger-fucked Taylor, first in the pussy, then in the ass, back and forth, wetter and deeper each time. Taylor could barely speak.

"Oh . . . I used to imagine tying you up and licking you everywhere until you begged me to come—and promised to be a good girl!—and do whatever I said, anytime, anywhere . . . lick my pussy in the girls' shower room, go beneath the football bleachers at night and finger-fuck me under my cheerleader skirt during the game . . . oh!"

"Mmm . . . I would have, too! But this is one of my old fantasies . . . I get you drunk and alone in the car, ah! I'm gonna taste you now—" Cindy's quick tongue and experienced mouth moved lower. She ripped off Taylor's tiny panties and threw them in the back seat, pulling her thighs even wider apart. Luscious pink showed wetly through dark blonde curls. Taylor placed one knee against the window and her other foot against the driver's window. Just like back in my cheerleading days, she thought, an incongruous giggle bursting from her lips, turning into a moan as Cindy's tongue and lips played with her clitoris while fingers entered her pussy and tight little asshole simultaneously, the other hand rhythmically pinching her nipples.

"Yes! Oh, yes, I'm gonna—" Taylor screamed in the car.

"Oh no, nooo!" A moist chuckle escaped Cindy's lips as she came up and kissed Taylor so deeply it left her gasping and limp. "You were always in control back then, Taylor—top cunt. But that's me, now!"

Taylor moaned desperately but Cindy would not relent. Her hands were stripping off her pale blue satin French panties and pushup bra. Then she climbed up, straddling Taylor's hips. She grasped Taylor's perfectly streaked blonde head and pulled her mouth hard onto her pussy.

"Now lick! Oh good, mmm, yes!" Cindy squeezed her own breasts and pinched her nipples while Taylor licked and sucked and slid her lips up and down Cindy's now soaking wet pussy. Then Cindy leaned down to tease Taylor's lovely blonde pussy with one hand, wanting to hear her moan with her face wet from Cindy's pussy. Cindy refused to let the little blonde cunt come yet, though. Oh no. But Cindy could come, yes!

"Ahh! Oh lick it, baby!" Cindy arched her hips and pushed her aching pussy harder into Taylor's eager mouth. Taylor suddenly plunged her fingers into Cindy's pulsing pussy and asshole together, pushing deeply in and out which prolonged Cindy's orgasm on and on, then started another orgasm straight on the heels of the first. Taylor grinned to herself. Ha! Cindy's not the only one with a little experience at licking panties! She giggled, and moaned again as Cindy's fingers found her own swollen and needy clitoris. Why won't she let me come? Taylor wondered, holding Cindy's bucking, writhing body to her mouth, licking and fucking her on and on, refusing to let go until every orgasm she could get was wrung out of her lithe body.

Taylor stopped, gasping, as Cindy's body finally draped across hers. Taylor pushed Cindy's hand against her almost painfully excited clitoris, just to hear one word.

"No."

Taylor's green eyes were dark and wild in the dimness. The smell of sex was intoxicating, enveloping them both in the slightly cramped space of the car.

Cindy giggled. "Oh baby, don't worry. You're going to have the best come you've ever had!"

Then Cindy's strong little arms were pushing Taylor's head down to the front floor of the vehicle while simultaneously pushing the car seat back as far as it would go.

"Wait a minute—" Taylor tried to say, but next thing she knew, her head was down on the soft carpeted floor of the car. Her legs were spread wide, then spread wider by Cindy's insistent hands which were already stroking and entering her front and back, as an unseen tongue licked across her anus and clitoris until her body was vibrating with excitement.

"Cindy," she moaned in a somewhat muffled voice. "I can't come like this!"

"You'll come for me, baby. This is my pussy, now!" Cindy's excitement was palpable, and Taylor's thoughts receded as tremors of pleasure curled her toes, made her thighs quiver, and her head feel like it'd explode. Taylor's belly clenched with an unbearable ecstasy, the feeling moving outward in a powerfully deep wave of sensual feeling, until her head and pussy both exploded.

"Ahh!" The vehicle reverberated with her scream and shook as her feet pounded the sides. Cindy's hard arms clenched around her hips, pulling her pussy inexorably into her busy mouth, licking and finger-fucking her until all she knew was pleasure, plunging through her bones, scissoring inside her vagina, oozing from her nipples . . . pleasure.

Afterward, when Cindy finally released Taylor from her tongue-lashing, she helped her into a seat. They held each other, quietly running hands and fingers with abandon all over and inside each other's bodies. There were no boundaries. Just bodies, and skin, and lips.

And tonight.

CALLIE'S LOVE STORY

MERINA CANYON

MARNIE FELL IN love with me before she even laid eyes on me. We met only once up here in the hills of West Virginia, and when she left, she took my country-girl heart with her.

She was sitting at the kitchen table when I walked into Jolene and Debby's cabin. She looked at me through those rose-colored glasses and I stopped in my tracks. Then she took off the glasses and revealed these blazing green-gold eyes like she almost couldn't believe the sight of me.

Jolene piped up and said, "Callie, this is Marnie—she's a writer from California." I knew other things were being said but I didn't hear anything else. I stared right back at Marnie and broke into a grin.

"I'm Callie," I said like an idiot.

"Yes," she said. "Yes, you are."

She had come out from California with a friend of hers, Sue Bancroft, and Sue was friends with my good buddies, Jolene and Debby. So I came over to their cabin (which they had built themselves) and there she was like she was just waiting for me.

Jolene and Debby started serving us all dinner, Debby's famous authentic southwest enchiladas. (She's half Mexican with dark hair and eyes.) I sat down across the table from this new bright-eyed California woman and forgot my manners. I barely said hey to Sue on my right. She was talking and Jolene was talking and Debby was rustling around, and Marnie and I just gazed at each other.

Finally, Marnie said, "I dreamed you."

"You can dream me anytime, darlin'," I said and then felt red faced.

"No, really," she said. "I had a dream that I would meet you on this trip."

"Are you sure it was me?" Lord, I sounded stupid.

"Your blue eyes give you away," she said. "I met you in a dream and looked into your crystal blue eyes."

"What did you see there?"

"Something very important," she said. "Something I *need*."

And suddenly Debby was dishing up more enchiladas and breaking the spell. As a matter of fact, I think she intended to break the spell. Break us up before we even got started. Even though Debby was just as good as married to Jolene, I still to this day believe she was crushed on Marnie from the get-go—the way she hovered around her like a bee to a flower.

And then there was Jolene. She might have been mad at me too because she expected Marnie and Sue to get together, even though they were obviously just friends. Lord, the tension was thick in that backwoods kitchen that night.

But I didn't care who was mad. If Marnie had dreamed me and saw something she *needed* in my eyes, I was prepared for her to jump right into my baby blues and wrap her arms and legs around me. She was a good-looking woman with long brown hair and delicious tanned legs. I felt like a country bumpkin, a tall, lean one with a short-short haircut, but Marnie must have thought I was the best thing she had seen in a long time.

She barely took her eyes off me, and when she tried to eat some enchilada, she kept smiling to herself—like she was amused by her own thoughts.

Sue was talking about sharks or something—she was a marine biologist I think, and Jolene and Debby paid her a lot of attention. That left Marnie and me to just eat each other up. I even had my foot searching for her foot under the table but kept bumping into Debby by mistake.

The Chianti was going around but I was afraid to drink it. Afraid I'd forget what I was doing and get silly drunk. So I let that ruby red wine sit in my glass. Marnie took baby sips off hers.

"If you say so, sugar," I said.

"Look," Debby said, "I'm tired of you two gawking at each other. Callie, you're going to do the dishes." She flashed her dark eyes at me.

"Aw, gee," I said. "Sure I will, Debby. I'm a heck of a dishwasher." I got up and started gathering dishes and Jolene got up too and we did it together.

It didn't take too long. I could hear Debby asking Marnie questions about writing novels and Marnie answering in short sentences. Marnie's voice was low and husky and I found myself straining to hear her every word about plot and characters and finding your muse.

With the dishes done and put away, we all went out to sit on the porch. It was still light out but getting dark. Right away Debby sat up close to Marnie in the porch swing and I had to sit on the steps.

Jolene and Sue were old college roommates so they were sitting in the two rocking chairs talking about the way it used to be. I wasn't paying attention to them. It may sound weird, but I could feel Marnie thinking about me. Our eyes couldn't meet anymore, what with everyone between us and it almost dark, but I swear I could feel her eyes, her thoughts, her *needs*, and it made me throb between my legs. I hadn't noticed anybody giving me a second look ever since Tawnya, and we had broken up more than a year before that. Being *needed* was totally irresistible and I started in on my own fantasy of making love to Marnie right then and there. I kept seeing those brown legs wrap around me, me slowly pulling her shirt off her, a kiss begging to happen, and me boldly holding it back until . . .

"You still over there, Callie?" Jolene said. It had gotten dark and I hadn't moved a muscle.

"Sure am," I said.

"You're so quiet I thought you'd fallen asleep," Jolene said.

"Just dreaming," I said.

Then I heard Marnie saying something about the car—had to go after something she left in the car—which was parked down the hill next to my jeep. My heart jumped. I sensed an opportunity.

"Take a light," Jolene said, and then Marnie brushed by me, casting a beam of light on my hands. She didn't say anything to me, but I felt her silent call, and after the beam of light went on down the path, I waited about one minute and tried to stand up without making a sound and follow her.

"Where ya'll going?" Debby demanded.

"Be back," I said and just kept going toward that beam of light.

When I got down to the cars, Marnie was leaning against my jeep with her head thrown back looking at the sky. There was a sliver of moon and a big star lighting her face.

I didn't know what to say. I put my right hand out in front of me, and without her turning to look, she put her hand out to meet mine. I thought, Our hands already met, and laughed a little.

She pulled my hand ever so gently to her and my whole body came with it. Now I was leaning into her. Our bodies connected and I felt my heart beating hard.

"You're my *other*," she whispered.

I wanted to say *Other what?* but I just said, "Yes, I am."

She laughed a little. "I'm so glad, so very glad to have found you."

"Mmm . . ." I replied. My hands floated around her hair and her shoulders.

She had her hands on the small of my back, moving them just a little, and I could feel how she wanted to kiss me. But I held back. I wanted to make her wait. A first kiss deserves to be a really good one. I knew already I'd never forget it.

"Please," she said. She was trembling slightly. I thought I felt her heart against my chest. I lightly circled her breasts with my fingertips.

"Dream lover," she said, "how I have needed you."

Her hands touched my face, traced my lips, and I kissed her fingertips. "Darlin'," I whispered back, "you've got me now."

"Please, Callie," she said. "I need to feel how you love me."

"I do love you," I said meekly. But how could I love her so fast? It didn't matter. Call it love at first sight. Call it crazy. Marnie was in love with me and I was flat out crazy for her.

I brought my lips as close to her lips without touching.

"Please," she said.

And I kissed her. Now this kiss wasn't about lips touching, not really. I mean, it went way beyond that. At first I thought Marnie had mistaken me for someone else, someone she had dreamed up and accidentally thought was me.

But then I knew. I didn't know what to call it. It was an urgent call to fall into each other and there was no holding back. We were both trembling and crying and kissing one long deep kiss—as though there was life passing between us—something sacred and magical and completely natural at the same time. It felt like there was a hole in the center of the universe and we were free-falling.

I can't remember all the moves we made now, but when Debby's voice called out down the hill, my hands were inside Marnic's shirt holding her breasts, and her hands were on my shoulders pulling me closer.

If Debby hadn't yelled out, "What's going on down there?" I think we would have gotten our clothes off in the next minute. But there was a big light coming our way, and we looked at each other in the night. Her eyes sparkled, wet with an urgent plea, and I felt her cheeks and realized they were wet with tears.

"Never leave me, Callie," she whispered. "I need you."

"Darlin'," I started, but now Debby was right up on us shining that blinding light in our faces.

"Oh, so that's it," Debby said sounding personally offended. She didn't lower the light. "Callie, you better be getting on home. It's late."

That made me hold Marnie tighter.

"It's OK," Marnie said. "I'm going on up."

That surprised me. Marnie turned toward Debby's light, buttoning up her shirt, and left me standing in the dark. The two of them rustled back up the hill. Should I follow? Or should I wait for her to slip away and come back to me? I didn't know what to do so I sat in my jeep and felt her kiss on my lips and envisioned how we made this hole in the universe where we both fell through. I'd never even thought such a feeling was possible.

I stayed in my jeep the whole night sitting up with my hand on the gear shift. I slept a little, dreamed Marnie came back to me. Nothing held us back in this dream and it felt so real that when I woke up I wasn't sure whether it had happened or not. Marnie was inside me—like she was living and breathing inside me.

I knew right then that my life had changed forever.

I started my jeep at first light. I figured I'd go on home and get cleaned up, feed the dogs and cats, come back later with flowers from Beckman's greenhouse. What would I say to Marnie when I saw her again? That I'd do anything to give her what she needed?

Driving out to my place an hour away, I remembered that in the dream, Marnie had said, "My muse." She said it into my ear as I slid two fingers inside her. I didn't really know what the word meant to her, but I would be her muse any day.

Now here's the hard part. After I got cleaned up and took care of the chores and all, and after I drove back out there with red roses, I just about died. Marnie and Sue were already gone.

"Left at noon," Jolene said. "Drove on to New York, then back out west."

I sort of collapsed on the steps right where I had sat the night before and started crying, my "beautiful" hands covering up my face. Jolene sat down beside me and picked up the roses. "I'm sorry, honey," she said, rubbing my back a little. "You liked that woman."

"I love her," I blurted out. "How could she leave without telling me good-bye?"

Jolene said, "She did seem funny about leaving. Kept looking around like she wasn't sure what to do."

"Jolie, you know she wanted *me*—not Sue."

"Yeah, I could see that," Jolene said. "It hurt Sue, so I wasn't happy about it. But now it's hurting you and I ain't happy about that either."

"Oh god," I said.

"Look," Jolene said, passing me a piece of paper, "she left us her address. Said to write. She likes letters she said."

I reached out for the address and saw how my hands were shaking.

"Poor baby," Jolene said and hugged me a little.

That piece of paper was all I had to connect me to Marnie, just that and my memory. I vowed to write her the most romantic letter I possibly could.

I heard Debby clinking around inside the cabin. Suddenly I felt sorry for her. She loved Marnie too, but Marnie chose me, not her or anybody else. Marnie saw something she needed in *my* eyes and I was the one she begged to kiss her.

"Keep the flowers," I said to Jolene. And I got up to head on home.

◆

THE FIRST LETTER I wrote probably sounded timid. I started doubting myself right away—maybe she was just playing around—said the same thing to all kinds of women—maybe even men! But no, even though I thought those thoughts, I knew for a fact that I, for one, had never felt anything like that *falling through the universe* before. And Marnie had tears on her face. It had to be real.

So I wrote the first letter and sent it to her home in California—it probably sat in her mailbox days before she even got home from her road trip with Sue. In the letter I said there was a light left burning in my heart for her—just about killed me that she had left without saying good-bye—she had changed me and I was keeping that light burning forever. I worried for two weeks waiting for an answer. I had those doubts crowding up in my mind but at the same time I had a fantastic energy running through me like magic. I was up at dawn every day rushing around with a smile on my face, doing chores and sailing through my work at the store. Couldn't wait to check that mailbox. Empty. I kept imagining what she was going to write back to me: *my muse, don't ever leave me.* And in my head I kept composing my next letter.

On a Saturday I walked down to the mailbox, about a quarter mile from my cabin. Bobby Joe was just putting the mail in my box when I rounded the corner. My heart jumped a little because I could see a distinct dusty rose-colored envelope in his hand along with my usual junk.

"Hey, Callie Brown," he said.

"Hey, Bobby Joe. Bring me some good news?"

"Always do. You know that." Then he drove off in his mail truck, kicking up a cloud of dust.

I held that envelope in my hand for what seemed like forever, my eyes tracing her letters that made up my name: *Callie Brown.* It made adrenalin run through my heart. She had written *my name.* Her handwriting looked artistic, like calligraphy or something. There was my rural route, town and state, zip code.

And then there was her return address: her own name!

I turned the envelope over. The flap was stuck tight and I thought about how it had to have passed over her tongue. I couldn't open it yet. I carried it back up the lane to my cabin and sat with it pressed to my heart while the dogs ran around and my cats tried to nuzzle into my lap.

And finally, I pried that flap open.

"My love, I have longed for you," her letter began, and I felt like I was falling through that hole in the universe again, spiraling into some great mystery that filled my heart with blazing light. Just those few words were all I needed. Marnie was in love with me.

◆

HER LETTER WAS short and I read it over and over, at least three times a day. I had it memorized on the first day, but I needed to see if there was anything hidden in the curves of her handwriting. The whole thing was such a mystery that I was sure there were all sorts of gems to be discovered.

We started sending letters back and forth, one per week—that's how long it took to get the mail from one side of the country to the other—from my mountain home to her mountain home. She had a phone, but I didn't, and to tell you the truth, I didn't want to call. I wanted those rose-colored envelopes to come so I could fire mine back. All week I'd catch myself composing in my head and at night I tried to get it down on yellow legal pads. By the time I sent my letter off, it might contain ten full pages.

Marnie's letters started out short, but by the second or third month her letters were getting longer and sometimes she'd send two in one week. She wrote about her magical dreams of me, how loving me made her so much closer to the mystery of life, how her heart was full of words to be written. She was a writer after all—a writer who needed to write if she was to breathe, and she was telling me that I was her muse. Me—a tall, strong mountain woman with calloused hands and big feet—I was the muse for a beautiful, radiant word-artist. The magnetic pull between us was agonizing but delicious.

We began to write about seeing each other again and being alone at last. It was a terrifying thought for me, but I began to live for it.

✦

WE PICKED A date: May 25th, 1985—my birthday. She was going to gift me with a plane ticket to San Francisco and she was going to pick me up and drive me to her mountain home. All day stocking the grocery store shelves I'd dream about touching her again. It felt so real that my fingertips and lips seemed to register tactile contact. My boss, Ernie, would yell at me: "Speed it up, Brownie!" and I'd shrug him off and retreat to the backroom for more privacy.

About that time I started receiving the novel. What I mean is, Marnie was sending me handwritten pages of her latest novel. She'd write them in the morning about five pages at a time, run them through a copy machine and send me the originals. It was a love story about two women madly in love who can't be together because of all sorts of obstacles in their path. She even gave the characters our names—Callie and Marnie—reversed the clock about a hundred years, and had us living somewhere in the British Isles—maybe Ireland although she confessed she wasn't sure.

My character was a tall, handsome landowner who loved to ride horses across the rolling green hills in the morning mist. Her character was a mysterious woman living with her husband on a dairy farm where she liked to sit at her bedroom window playing a Celtic harp in the night breezes. These two lovers had a secret hiding place in the forest where they met a couple times a week. When the Marnie character turns up pregnant, she insists that the baby belongs to Callie, not to her husband. Callie refuses to believe such a thing is possible and storms off on her horse. The longing for each other only intensifies, Callie racing through the morning mist and Marnie playing sad harp melodies on the night breezes.

While stocking the grocery store shelves, I began to wonder if two women could maybe conceive a child together. Could love and longing be so powerful as to set off a life-creating chemical chain reaction? Whatever the case, I had my own story going on in my head about how I would build a beautiful log cabin for Marnie and me. I'd raise horses while Marnie wrote her novels. I'd build her a tree house/writing studio—I even started to draw up the plans. Although I was only a grocery store stock person, I knew I had the talent to be a builder, and suddenly my heart was on fire to design a dream house for the love of my life. I read architecture books from the library and talked to every person I knew who had built their own place, including Jolene.

Jolene was a big comfort to me in those days. I'd stop by her cabin when I knew Debby was working at the restaurant. I'd ask Jolene to tell me again how she'd taken down all those trees and made that cabin, but the conversation always found its way back to Marnie.

Jolene would sit in the rocker on the porch while I swung crooked in the porch swing. She seemed so wise sitting there barely swaying in the rocker, looking out down the hill as though she were waiting for something.

"That woman has seized your heart," Jolene said one day.

"Don't I know it," I said dumbly. I craved to talk about Marnie.

"You think you're going to get her out here, or are you going to move out west?"

"I don't know," I confessed. "Hell, I don't know one day from the next."

"Long-distance relationships are hard to keep up," she added.

"But we plan to see each other," I said desperately. "You know—in May like I told you before."

"I know what you told me, Callie, but there's a long, cold winter between now and then, and who's going to keep you warm at night?"

"Marnie sleeps with me every night in my heart," I said. I felt my face turn fire red.

"Uh huh," Jolene said.

That's when I heard Debby's truck rumbling up the hill and said, "I better get on home."

"Come back soon, you lovesick puppy," Jolene said, and I said I would.

◆

A LONG, COLD winter. That's right. Somehow I had to get through all those cords of wood and keep chopping and shoveling snow and stocking grocery store shelves before I could see my lover again. The letters started coming less and the novel pages started coming more. Marnie's character had the baby—a beautiful little girl with crystal blue eyes like mine. In a letter, Marnie asked me to name the new character and I chose Heather because it made me think of a romantic scenario in Ireland. My character was still believing that the baby wasn't hers and kept storming off at a gallop on her fast horse. Marnie's character was suffering deeply from intense longing. She loved the child and created plenty of beautiful harp music, but she was losing her mind over Callie rejecting her. Marnie's housekeeper in the novel, a young blonde woman named Fay was falling in love with Marnie and was at her side constantly. The young housekeeper knew all about Callie because Marnie would confide in her and cry in her arms at night.

That's when I got jealous. I was suddenly suspicious. Who was this housekeeper named Fay? Was she just a character in the novel or did she actually exist? I couldn't tell. The husband of the Marnie character was pure fiction—I was pretty sure of that. But I wasn't so sure about this Fay. She seemed real to me. I could see her. She was thin and whispery and quivery like a fairy. And I could feel how much she loved my Marnie. Yes, I was jealous of someone else being with Marnie even if that person was madeup. Suddenly it didn't make a bit of difference. I was mad, and my anger helped me chop a lot more wood in January. My building plans came to a standstill, and I decided to punish Marnie by not writing for a whole week. Then I extended it to ten days to make more of an impression.

The pages of the novel kept coming, up to twenty-five pages per week—and there was a problem. Not only was my character starting to show an interest in another woman in my employ, but the kid, Heather, was sick with a mysterious illness. Marnie was scared to death that the child would die. Even though the Marnie character claimed that the baby belonged to the Callie character, I couldn't get myself to feel bad for the kid. I was still dwelling on this blonde demon Fay character always there in the shadows ready to be of service in any way to Marnie. Dammit. I should have been there! But that's when I realized that Marnie, the real woman, was way out of my league. She was a writer, a California mystic, a radiant woman oozing with sensuality. I was just a long, tall country hick with nothing to offer. Maybe she *thought* she loved me, but if she ever had a chance to be with me, she'd see the truth. Yes, I was scared but mostly I was mad. I wrote back shorter letters about winter chores and didn't say too much about missing her or about our planned rendezvous in May. Meanwhile the kid got sicker and sicker, with the Marnie character scrambling for remedies.

That's when I met Roseanne. She came into the store one day in February. I'd seen her before but I hadn't paid much attention til that day. She was holding Braeburn apples in her hands but she was looking at me as though she were tasting *me*. I was on a step stool reaching the overflow shelf, and when I saw her looking at me, I grinned at her, and she said, "Hey, Callie."

"Well, hey," I said too friendly. I was surprised she knew my name but then turned red faced when I realized I was wearing my name on my shirt like a heart on a sleeve.

"How tall *are* you?" she asked, still holding those red apples.

"Five ten and a half," I said too proudly. "And you?" God, I sounded dumb.

She laughed. "Oh, I'm five foot four or five—can't remember which."

Damn! She struck me as awful cute as she wandered around the produce section knowing that my eyes were still on her. Finally, she came back around to where I was standing with my arms crossed.

I said, "You want to get something to eat? I'll be done here in an hour."

That's when she turned red and said, "Yes. Yes, I'd like that."

The only café close by was the Mexican one where Debby worked. Hell, didn't make any difference. Roseanne and I sat across from each other at a table too small for both us and the plates.

"I've seen you a lot of times in the store," Roseanne said.

"You have?" I knew I sounded like an idiot.

"Yeah—you're always looking so strong and handy."

I beamed with pride when she said that.

"But," she continued, "you're always a million miles away. Today's the first time I caught your attention." She smiled, cute.

I thought of telling her about Marnie and what kind of hell I'd been through lately, but I didn't want to talk about Marnie anymore. I just wanted to flirt with Roseanne.

She told me she had just gone through a divorce. Her husband was a brute and a cheater and he'd hit her hard on more than one occasion. Hearing that, I wanted to go after that asshole and pound him into the ground like a fence post. What could make a man hit a pretty flower like Roseanne?

Debby waited on us—it was early and we were the only customers.

"Hey, Callie," she said, sour-pussed. "Didn't know you knew Roseanne." She raised her eyebrows a little too high.

"Didn't until today," I said, grinning at Roseanne. I wanted to reach for her hand.

"How's Marnie?" Debby said flatly.

I felt hot. I couldn't answer right away. I pretended to look at the menu.

"I said, how's Marnie?" Debby bore down on me.

"She's three thousand *fucking* miles away—that's how she is!" I noticed Roseanne push back some. She looked a little scared.

Debby took our order and went away and then I apologized to Roseanne.

"Sorry 'bout that. Debby and me's mad at each other is all."

"Who's Marnie?" Roseanne asked without looking at me.

"My ex," I said, and just then my heart caught in my throat. What had I done? Betrayed Marnie. But it served her right, didn't it?

◆

THAT NIGHT ALONE in my cabin I was in a panic. For the first time I wanted to call Marnie direct and ask her to forgive me. But I couldn't call. I was ten miles from a phone and it was snowing again. I suddenly got terrified that the kid, Heather, was going to die. Maybe she *did* belong to the Callie character after all. I started writing Marnie an urgent letter. *Please don't let the baby die. Please don't let the baby die.* I wrote it over and over and then wadded it up and threw it in the fire.

"Goddammit, Marnie!" I said out loud. "What's happening to me?" I cried and cried, all broken down on the floor. After a while I fell asleep with my dogs on top of me. *Please don't let the baby die* filtered in and out of my dreams.

◆

THE NEXT DAY was Saturday and I trudged through the deep snow to get to the mailbox. Bobby Joe hadn't come yet so I walked up and down the road to keep warm. I thought about how he might be stuck somewhere in that mail truck and my letter from Marnie would be lying there frozen. I set off down the road in the direction he would come. I must have walked a half mile before I found him trying to push and drive that truck at the same time.

"Callie Brown!" he called out, red faced. "Buddy, am I glad to see you!"

I wanted to ask for my mail first off but I knew I had to be helpful. The two of us dug out around the rear tire chains and then scattered sand. I pushed from the rear while he pushed from the driver's door. The truck finally started moving on forward and Bobby Joe yelled, "Get in, partner." He carried me on down to my mailbox and I hopped out.

"Don't forget my mail, Bobby Joe." I was too cold and tired to get red faced.

"Here it is." He pulled a rubber-banded bundle out of the back. "Hope it's good news."

I carried that bundle on up to my cabin and built up my fire so I could warm my hands before opening my letter.

It wasn't a letter. It was another installment of the novel, about ten pages, and suddenly I was scared to read it. "Please don't let the baby die," I cried and my tears dripped all over the pages. I couldn't piece the words together. All I could see was the curve of Marnie's handwriting and the names: Callie, Heather, Fay, and a new name—Rose. How could she pick *Rose* out of a hat?

That's when something reared up in me and I couldn't stand it anymore. I watched Marnie's handwriting burning up in the fire. "Please don't let the baby die," was all I could say.

Sunday morning I lay in bed like I was sick, and the dogs circled around and around the cabin til I finally got up and let them out. I was supposed to get into work that afternoon, and it was going to take some doing to get my jeep rolling.

My heart was hanging in my chest like a dead weight. I was miserable—didn't want to eat, couldn't call in sick 'cause I didn't have a phone. I started moving one foot in front of the other, and in an icy daze managed to feed the animals and get myself to work late at three thirty.

The boss just grunted at me. I could have said I was snowbound, but shit! I didn't care what Ernie thought. I went about my work with a frown frozen on my face and I couldn't change it. By four thirty a thawed tear dripped out of each eye, but there was no feeling attached to it. *Please don't let the baby die* wasn't even going through my head anymore.

"Hey, good lookin'. Why so sad?"

I turned from the bread shelves and saw Roseanne standing there in a red wool coat with an empty cart in front of her.

"Hey, Roseanne," I said meekly.

"What's wrong?" she asked all concerned.

"Somebody I know just died," I surprised myself by saying.

"That's awful, Callie honey. Who was it?"

I saw tears well up in Roseanne's eyes, just from looking at me I guess.

"I don't want to talk about it," I said flatly, scooting a loaf of Wonder Bread onto the shelf.

"Callie, you come to my house when you get off. I'll cook you supper. You like steak? Course you do. You come—promise?"

She was sweet on me all right, and now I wasn't sure I was interested, especially since she might just be a straight woman playing *lesbo* for half a week. But hell, laying down with a warm, pretty woman like that just might unfreeze me.

"OK," I said.

"You like chocolate cake?" she asked.

"Yeah," I said.

"Oh, good," she said and went on down the aisle.

◆

AND I DID lay down with Roseanne that night and the night after that and the night after that. She didn't have any trouble figuring out how to be with a woman—she said she had always wanted to but never met a lesbian close up before me. And now she was crazy about me, and so I set my heart before her fire to thaw out.

I didn't write to Marnie. Day after day went by and when envelopes arrived from her I chucked them right into the fireplace unopened. I felt a little sick when I did that—like I was going to throw up, but I'd remind myself that she was out of my league anyway and I'd never get her to move out here and I sure as hell wasn't moving to California. Jolene was right. Long-distance relationships were doomed.

◆

I WENT UP to see Jolene once the roads were clearer and the snowbanks were melting. I sat at her table while she served me tea.

"Look," she said, and reached for a long rose-colored envelope on the counter. "I got this letter from Marnie. She's been worried about you 'cause you don't write. I already wrote her back and told her you were OK."

I felt mad instantly. "What'd you tell her?" I snapped.

"That's all. That you were OK. She didn't write me again, but she did ask me to pass this postcard on to you."

I looked up and took the card from Jolene's hand. It had a picture of some misty Irish countryside. Marnie's handwriting made the letters for: *My love, you have left me.*

And yes, I had left her. I left the most magical woman I'd ever met and I wasn't even sure why. I never would find that hole in the universe again. And I never found out how the novel ended—did the kid die or did she get better? Did Marnie and Callie ride off into the sunset together? I don't know, but I went on to be happy in my own way, never ever forgetting that Marnie had fallen in love with me.

THE TALE OF A LESBIAN SLUT: HOW I MET AND MARRIED A NICE JEWISH DOCTOR *(MY MOTHER IS SO PROUD!)*, OR, HOW I BECAME MONOGAMOUS AND MARRIED

TATE O'BRIEN

INTRODUCTION

I WASN'T EVEN supposed to be on that boat.

My partner of nearly five years had just dumped me for someone new, saying she needed to be alone (which made no sense at all). I had to find a new place to live since the house was in her name. To top it all off, I'd recently resigned from my executive job, with no new prospects in sight.

I grieved the loss of my relationship and my job all through the summer, and then metaphorically took a deep breath and looked around.

Rather than sit around my new rental house moping and wearing an ever larger ass-shaped divot into my new couch, I decided to try my hand at the travel-writing gig. An online company offered a home study course on travel writing. I'd always loved to travel. Since I was a kid, I'd had a goal of visiting all fifty states. I'd just knocked Maine off my list the year before (number forty-eight) and had had the opportunity for a dream trip to Hawaii a few months prior (number forty-nine) for the wedding of two dear friends. Alaska was the only state that had escaped my regard.

What better way to launch a new career, I thought, than going on a lesbian cruise to Alaska? I'll interview the talent and the Olivia staff, maybe sell a few articles to queer magazines, and take the trip of a lifetime in the company of beautiful women. This is providence!

Embracing the spirit of spontaneity, I made all the arrangements for the cruise a mere three days before the boat was to depart, and off I went in my little silver Subaru. (Yes, I own a Subaru. After all, I am a lesbian.)

Driving twelve hundred miles in two days from Colorado to Seattle, I dropped my cat with my folks (Yes, I have a cat. I am a lesbian) and took the train to Vancouver, British Columbia. A minivan, a ferry, a train, and the subway were insufficient to get me to the ship: I also had to walk over a mile hauling a hundred pounds of gear and literature to board the *ms Statendam*, a Holland America ship fully chartered by the lesbians of Olivia.

I wasn't looking for love on the boat. I was, I admit, looking for some inspired writing, some fun, and some sex, in that order. The last, I anticipated, would involve more than one lucky lady. You know, since I'd recently become available and all.

My first day on the ship I was understandably sleep deprived, and the afternoon passed in a blur of lifeboat drills, orientations, dinner, and a show. I was pooped. So after all that I said good-bye to my new friends Patty and Emily and took myself off to bed by eleven p.m. No partying for me. I needed my beauty sleep.

I was awakened at 6:00 a.m. by the captain announcing the sight of orcas off the port bow. Of course, I dragged my fleece on and went up on deck just in time to see a single spout. The vista was breathtaking. Although I stood there for another fifteen minutes straining my eyes, I experienced nothing more but cold ocean air blowing through my hastily donned and thoroughly inadequate garments, so I hustled back inside.

By then completely awake, I got dressed, had some breakfast, and went to the ship gym, which had dazzling wraparound views of the inside passage. Deep green pines soared up cliffsides on an endless series of pristine islands. Bald eagles perched on treetops. The water was a smooth and beautiful turquoise reflecting both the sky and a few errant white clouds.

The first time I laid eyes on Dr. Laura Cohen of Washington, DC, was at lunch that day: She was sitting against a brilliant backdrop of bright ocean and sky.

Olivia, being a very considerate and sensitive company, had orchestrated a series of solo events for those traveling without companionship. I had already attended two solo activities, and enjoyed meeting some friendly women. At our first lunch, I was supposed to be seated with a group from the Mountain States Solos, but somehow I stopped at Laura's table (Mid-Atlantic) and couldn't force myself to leave. I even asked the courteous dining room staff for an extra chair and setting, since the table was already full of other lesbians.

Laura was wearing a blue fleece shirt that brought out the color of her eyes perfectly, I noticed right away. She was chatty, polite, and very concerned about organizing a party later that afternoon at the Crow's Nest, the bar on the top of the ship. She must have asked seven or eight times if folks were going to meet at the Crow's Nest at 2:45 p.m.

After lunch, I went to a solos' line-dancing lesson, and then met the group from lunch at 2:45 p.m. in the Crow's Nest. The Nest featured panoramic views: the skies were now cloudy, but the islands and water were wild and gorgeous. Before long, Laura showed up looking happy to see everyone. She practically glowed. Little did I know at this point that Laura had arranged the get-together solely in order to see me again.

Seven or eight women showed up in the Nest before we started ordering drinks, including my new friends Patty and Emily. We started, at Emily's request, with shots of tequila and margaritas all around. Inevitable drunkenness occurred.

Then Emily let us all in on a little secret: her friends from New York City had bet her money that she couldn't kiss eight women while on the cruise, one for each day. Laura, being the helpful woman that she was, offered to get Emily started on the right foot with a little smooch. Everyone hooted and cheered. Then a light bulb went off in my drunken head: I could kiss Emily, too! But somehow, my attention was diverted by Laura. I boldly crossed over to Laura's seat and asked her if I could kiss her instead. This was the smartest decision I'd ever made, despite the fact that I was six drinks in at this point.

When I leaned in to kiss Laura, it was as if time came to a

screeching halt. It wasn't even a French kiss, but when I pulled back from her mouth, I felt like the world had started anew. Then Laura pulled away, her eyes averted, and I was concerned. Wow, I thought, there's a new reaction. Usually girls like it when I kiss them.

The rest of the afternoon passed in a haze of flirtation and fun. Patty, Emily, Laura, and I decided to go together to the evening show and have dinner afterward. Laura needed to change, and asked me if I wanted to walk her to her cabin before meeting everyone in the showroom. I was intrigued: perhaps she wasn't taken aback by my kiss after all. Sure enough, when we got to her stateroom, Laura kissed me again. It was wonderful. I felt elated! I mean, really, Laura was one hot number, and she was dialing mine.

The four of us had such fun drinking and taking silly photos that the show featuring Kate Clinton was even more hilarious than usual. Afterward, we met up with some more ladies in the Crow's Nest.

My sharpest memory of that evening is of riding the elevator down from the Nest with Patty and Laura. Laura's room was on a floor higher and Patty's room on a floor lower than mine. When the elevator stopped for Laura, despite the kisses and the flirting that afternoon, Laura got off the elevator without so much as a hug for me. I stood rooted to the carpet for several seconds in surprise, until the elevator doors started to close. Then I made a highly impulsive decision and leapt between the doors without a word to Patty, hoping that Laura would at least give me a quick kiss if no one were watching. Instead, she turned and started walking toward her door. Perplexed, I followed, thinking that maybe I would walk her to her door, and get a goodnight kiss there. Instead, she opened the door to the room and invited me inside. Still no kiss. But I was drunk and confused, and totally willing to follow the lead of this attractive, intriguing woman, so I entered, not looking back. I stayed for several hours.

We didn't make any plans together for the next day. As I wandered back to my room later, I remember thinking that I would love to see Laura again, but that I would allow the universe to take me where it would.

I woke up the next morning excited to be going on my first excursion. Excursions were preplanned activities off the ship, available each day the ship was in port. For my very first day in Juneau, I had scheduled a snorkeling trip to complement the snorkeling I'd just done in Hawaii (warm, clear water, colorful fish, sandy beaches, and chicks in bikinis). I wanted to see how different it would be. Was it ever!

First, we put on full wetsuits, gloves, booties, and hoods. Then we schlepped down to the rocky coast and hiked down slick rocks until we reached the edge of the freezing surf. The water was ice cold with visibility of less than four feet. Fun. Despite the challenges, though, I had a great time. We saw primarily invertebrates, and because we were snorkeling at the lowest tide of the month, we saw lots of creatures that other visitors to Alaska only dream of.

When the snorkeling adventure was over, we still had a few hours before the ship would sail, so I wandered around town shopping and snapping photos. I must admit at this point that I have a funny little tradition. Whenever I'm in a gift shop or truck stop, I automatically look for my name on the key chains, miniature license plates, coffee mugs, or whatever they have on sale. Since I have sort of a rare name, I've not ever found a tchotchke for myself. But that day I did find a cute key chain with Laura's name on it. Feeling a little sheepish, I bought it for her.

At this point I'd like to pause the love story for an amusing anecdote. While touring Juneau, I ran into two Olivia staff members who were also touring. I'd met them in the course of my journalistic work while setting up interviews with the owner of the company and some of the performers.

The three of us were standing by an inlet on the boardwalk when I pointed to the fish swimming below and inquired as to their species. The women politely responded that the salmon were running upstream to spawn, and we made more small talk, mostly about their jobs and the articles for which I was gathering info. I looked down, and suddenly saw this huge shape gliding through the water. Stunned, I exclaimed, "That's the biggest fish I've ever seen! Holy cow! That salmon is as big as I am! It must be over a hundred pounds!" I was very excited. I pointed and jumped up and down on the wooden planks, making hollow, thudding noises.

I think those two women must have hurt their insides laughing at me. When they finally managed to start breathing again, I heard, "Tate. That's not a salmon, that's a seal." Seals eat fish. I knew that.

My reputation with the staff, though, as an informed, cool observer of the world around me, was totally blown. I looked like a rube. And of course the story spread once we were all back on the ship. How embarrassing.

Now, back to our love story. When I reboarded the ship that afternoon, I retraced my steps to Laura's cabin, hoping I'd remembered the number correctly in my drunken stupor of the previous evening, and that she wouldn't be back on the ship yet. I didn't want to get caught doing a silly, romantic thing. I felt like I was back in junior high school. I didn't want anyone to see me, to judge me, to think that I had a girlish crush, which, of course, I did.

With several cautious glances up and down the corridor, I nervously twist-tied the key chain to the doorknob and then ran away, not knowing what Laura would do should she find the gift attached to what I hoped was her door.

A few minutes later Laura called. My heart pounding, I made a date with her for the Crow's Nest later that afternoon, and that night passed much the same way the previous night had, with a show, dinner, and partying in the Crow's Nest with the same cast of characters. The only difference: Laura visited my stateroom this time.

Each day flew past with the same itinerary: separate excursions for Laura and me in the morning that we had each planned in advance (Hiking! Canoeing! Zip-lining! Glacier trekking! Wildlife viewing! Shopping!), drinking in the Nest in the afternoon followed by an evening of debauchery with friends, and a warm night in the arms of my new love interest. I loved living in the moment, savoring the juices from each day.

Before long, it seemed, it was the final full day on board the ship. Our last day was at sea, so instead of excursioning, we all (say it with me now) met in the Crow's Nest for drinks. I found myself feeling pensive. I repeated to myself, Tasha, this is just a shipboard romance. Let it go. You don't have to have anything with this woman but the moment. But I didn't want to let it go. I liked this woman Laura; I liked her a lot. We talked of things both deep and shallow, we had tons in common, we'd had great fun by ourselves and with others, and I never felt a sense of obligation or worry about being with her. And, she was a PhD statistician . . . a doctor!

Another brief sidenote: Laura and I were the talk of the cruise. Despite our efforts to be discreet, every woman on board seemed interested in our comings and goings. Random women I'd never met would walk up to me without preamble and ask, "So which one of you is moving?" Who the hell are you? I'd think. "No one's moving anywhere," I would forcefully iterate. And believe. Mostly.

I didn't know if I liked Laura for herself, or just because we'd had such a good time on vacation. I'd been tricked by vacation romances before, you see, and I didn't much like it, so when Laura invited me to spend the next night with her in Anchorage instead of at the hotel I had reserved for myself, I was hesitant.

"Is this a good idea?" I asked Laura.

"Of course it is," she said.

So I stayed with her. It worked out well.

Leaving her in Anchorage was very hard. Laura was off on a Denali adventure, and I was headed back to Seattle and my cat.

I texted her before my flight took off. I texted her when I landed in Seattle. She called me from her hotel that night in Denali, gazing at the Northern Lights and whispering sweet things in my ear. We continued to bond via phone.

The unexpected litmus test of our relationship came while I was still in Seattle. Each night we would chat on the phone after Laura was done with her activities in Denali. And each time I would be lying on my bed at my parents' house in Seattle. And each time my cat, Bubba, would crawl up on my chest, bump the phone with her head, and start purring to wake the dead. Every single time. Understand that Bubba was not a purring cat. This was highly unusual, some might even say unprecedented, behavior on her part. It seemed clear that Bubba wanted Laura for her new mommy.

When I returned home to Colorado, the kitty behavior continued right along with the daily phone calls.

I guess I was starry eyed, because I asked every friend some variation of the question about moving. Some even teased me by saying I was going to marry this woman and have her babies. I told all those people (approximately forty-two of them) that they were all insane, that I hated DC and would never live there, and that I didn't believe in marriage anyhow, so bug off.

Finally, I broached the subject of a DC visit with Laura. I was worried and nervous. I asked Laura, "What if I visit, and we spend a lot of time together, and I like you too much?" I was truly concerned.

Laura just laughed. "That would be just fine," she reassured. And it was fine.

We dated for a few months, and then had the dreaded relationship conversation. What form would our relationship take? I'd pretty much been polyamorous in all my past significant relationships, and I was pretty sure that worked for me. Laura had always been monogamous and had never considered anything else. We had ourselves a dilemma, and it was a deal breaker if we couldn't reach agreement.

We (being good lesbians) processed, talked, discussed, and debated all the available options. Laura considered a more open form, even though it made her a bit uncomfortable to be exploring new territory. I really listened to what she had to say, and tried to think about whether being in a closed form would make me feel trapped. This conversation took several weeks and spanned several states. After all that, in the end, when it came down to brass tacks, I realized that I only wanted to be with Laura. I really, honestly, truly, just wanted to be with this one woman. I would have been more surprised, but it felt so right. And Laura agreed.

That's how this poly-girl became a mono-girl.

After months of flying weekly between Colorado and Washington, DC, Laura and I made the decision to live together.

Let me elaborate: After knowing this woman for a mere four months, I decided to move across the country, leaving behind everyone and everything I knew. It wasn't a lesbian Internet hookup, at least, but how much better is a lesbian cruise hookup? I didn't plan to rent a (lesbian) U-Haul only because Laura had hurt her shoulder and couldn't help unload in DC.

Laura was old-fashioned. She insisted that before we move in together that we meet each other's families. I was skeptical. Laura didn't budge. None of my previous girlfriends had ever wanted that. In fact, my most recent ex had refused to meet my family until we had been dating almost three years. (Perhaps that should have been a clue, but I missed it.)

Laura won the debate. We flew to Seattle and Florida and met everyone. Our families loved our respective girlfriends, it all worked out just fine, and I had worried needlessly. Laura was right. Again.

The biggest surprise of all: After living together for several months, I asked Laura to marry me. As corny as it sounds, every time I looked inside my heart, I saw Laura there holding my hand. I wanted that to last forever.

When it came time to propose, I wracked my brain for a creative, romantic, fabulous way to ask Laura to marry me.

I'd never before seriously considered marrying someone. Neither of us had ever been engaged, let alone married. I wanted it to be special. On impulse (are we seeing a trend here?), I asked Laura to marry me on the JumboTron screen at the True Colors concert in front of thousands of partying queers. To my utter surprise, Laura was for once in her life completely speechless. I had rendered her mute! When she finally got her head together, she said yes. I was so thrilled; I didn't stop smiling the whole night.

I was surprised by how happy it made me to hear her accept my proposal, especially since I had been antimarriage (as an oppressive, limiting form of ownership supporting institutional patriarchy and the devaluing of women) for my entire life. Somehow, it just felt right. What can I say?

After our whirlwind romance, we decided to be engaged for just over a year—just enough time for me to put my extensive event-planning to good use in throwing us one heck of a Colorado destination wedding for eighty friends and family. I'm happier than I ever imagined being in my life. I love being married, and I love my new wife.

That's one way to make a slut monogamous and married.